PAINTING FOR KEEPS

A Cupid Cafe story

LANDRA GRAF

Always hope!
Landra G

After Glows Publishing

Painting For Keeps

© Copyright 2016 Landra Graf

Published by After Glows

PO Box 224

Middleburg, FL 32050

AfterGlowsPublishing.com

Cover by LKO Designs

Formatting by AG Formatting

All rights reserved under the International and Pan-American Copyright Conventions. No part of this book may be reproduced or transmitted in any form or by any means, electronic or mechanical, including photocopying, recording, or by any information storage and retrieval system, without permission in writing from the publisher.

This is a work of fiction. Names, places, characters and incidents are either the product of the author's imagination or are used fictitiously, and any resemblance to any actual persons, living or dead, organizations, events or locales is entirely coincidental.

Painting For Keeps

An invitation to Cupid's Café will change your life.

Agatha, Aggie, Kakos lost her boyfriend, her apartment, and now, is one brownie bite away from purging her binge when an invitation to Cupid's Café shows up on her doorstep. Fighting bulimia and her mother's constant verbal abuse has never been easy, but this nutritionist is determined to be stronger than her weakest link. She'll meet a secret admirer at Cupid's for a morale booster, if nothing else.

Following a break-in and the destruction of his paintings, starving artist Murphy O'Shea finds himself at wit's end. Not only does he need to create twelve more paintings, but in the midst of another manic depressive episode, the challenge seems impossible. He's got two months or he'll have to cancel his first show. The Cupid's Café invite offers him a chance to find his muse. He doesn't expect it to be the woman he's mirrored the past two years paintings on, nor does he plan on being able to offer Aggie the help she needs.

Can they find a way to conquer their inner demons or will they succumb to the idea they aren't worth a happily ever after?

Chapter One

Which first? Agatha Kakos waffled, staring at the half pint of Häagen-Dazs and the box of Cosmic brownies. Should she eat either of these items? No, but after the day she lived through, falling off the wagon seemed the best approach. It sure beat drugs or alcohol, which she'd possessed no tolerance for. No, bingeing followed by purging topped her list as the drug of choice. Especially since the breakup was official, two years down the drain. She'd lost the other half of her. She found herself no longer part of an *us*. She was now a *numero uno*.

When Jordan had asked for a break a month before their scheduled move in date, she'd only seen the signs of pre-merging household jitters. It made sense. Hell, she'd experienced a few doubts herself about downsizing her own things and giving up her shared space. Then came their usual evenings spent together, canceled due to a big work project, followed by broken lunch dates paired with unreturned phone calls and texts. When she went to his office last week, his secretary told her he'd be in meetings all day. A finance analyst unavailable to his girlfriend, one he planned on moving in with?

She'd finally got the gumption that morning, pushing aside her fear due to the fact she was supposed to be out of her current apartment a week prior and knocked on his front door before work. They'd never exchanged keys during their relationship. A normal person might have viewed that as a warning sign. She'd thought it sweet he wanted to wait. Did he answer the door? Not *him*.

Instead, a twenty-something, thin framed, red headed knockout with long legs and a smile greeted her. She'd called out for Jordan, her pink heels clacking on the tile floor as she walked back into the apartment, leaving the door wide open.

Yep, the memory convinced Aggie to dip her spoon into the salted caramel ice cream and shove the bite into her mouth. Sugary goodness melted on her tongue, even as her stomach soured at the thought of the kiss. Young-hot-pink-heeled-gal locked lips with Jordan, a steamy ten-second-seems-like-forever kiss seared into her memory, complete with a lower lip nibble. Then the woman who'd replaced her announced Aggie's presence at the door.

Jordan barely bothered to look guilty when he approached her. Another salted caramel bite slid between her lips. The words *not compatible* were etched into her brain since he'd said them at least three times. He apologized for letting her find out like this, for still planning to move in to the duplex they purchased, but work kept him busy. Too busy to tell the woman he'd sent 'love ya, cuddles' text messages to every day for over a year they were over and everything she'd saved for physically and emotionally was gone like bait off a hook.

Who took over twelve months to commit to deeper feelings in a relationship? This guy. He'd reeled her in like one of those river monsters from the reality television show playing in the background on her flat screen. Slow, steady, and with a ton of false promises. Yet, she'd become a fool of a fish, falling for her captor and wanting to be kept.

One more spoonful and her belly reached acceptance mode, finally on board with dulling the pain through carbs. Then the ringtone "Maneater" by Hall and Oates echoed through the room. Curse her traitorous heart for wanting it to be Jordan, for wanting to call him, and instead, she got her mother.

She dragged herself off the couch and reached for the phone on the coffee table with a sigh. "Good evening, Edith."

"Evening, Agatha. You sound awful. I take it the talk with your boyfriend didn't go as planned?" Her mother had encouraged Aggie to grab the fish by the gills and talk to her ex days ago.

"You'd be right. Looks like we're not moving in together after all. He's found another roommate and needs a break." She needed to put a positive spin on this, even if coupled with white lies. "I planned to call you in the morning. I'm going to stay on a month-to-month contract at my current place and take some time to figure things out."

"Sure, dear, but figuring things out doesn't get you what you want. You obviously did something to scare him away. You're not bingeing again, are you?"

Aggie stopped mid-spoonful to her mouth. "Of course not."

"Strong women are fueled by their desire to be taken care of. You need to re-interest him."

"He cheated on me, Edith."

The tap of her mother's nails echoed through the phone. "Oh no, dear. Then he's not worth it. You need to get up, get dressed, go out and paint the town."

"I don't feel like strutting myself around."

"Back on the market is the only thing to do, Agatha. Find another man, richer, wiser. I've got to get ready for a charity dinner tonight, but I'll expect an update in a few days from you. Get a new man, reel him in, and make Jordan suffer."

After hanging up the phone, Aggie took notice of her entire rigid demeanor and forced her shoulders to relax and her muscles to loosen. Her mother never helped in a crisis. The woman had a knack for making things worse. She wouldn't rely on someone else. No, she'd survived over the years by being self-sufficient and relying on herself.

Depending on someone else came with a dose of trouble, evidenced with her boyfriend, now an ex, and the only thing to assuage her broken heart being the softened tub of ice cream and a box of Cosmic brownies. Yes, this time she'd start with a brownie and shoved half the frosted, candy-sprinkled goodness into her mouth.

The chocolate melted, doing the job she'd intended—it made her feel good. She let her mind focus on the television, allowing her bad habits to continue without thought. Swallowing the second half of the brownie, she reached for another. The crinkle of plastic for the tasty morsels' wrapping resonated through the room. The drone of the British television host speaking of challenges to his attempts at catching a big one continued. But as the chocolate of brownie number two touched her lips, another knock came at the door.

This one was heavier than Mrs. Sanders, her sixty-plus landlord, and she'd never tell a soul how she jumped up so fast, tossing the brownie into the small waste bucket, and nearly tripped on the leg of her coffee table. She'd also never mention her quick stop at the mirror hanging catty-corner from the door, wiping at the smudge of chocolate at the edge of her mouth, and smoothing her University of Louisville T-shirt to ensure no crumbs remained.

Thoughts of Jordan's desperate apologies, of his begging pleas asking her to take him back ran rampant in her mind, and when she opened the door, she held tightly to the wood, ready to slam the damn thing in his face to get her retribution. But he wasn't there to see her eager, roaring, vengeful resolve.

No, instead was a man in a brown button-down shirt and matching pants, UPS symbol blazing from the pocket on the shirt, a small handheld machine in one hand, a thin envelope in the other. "Delivery for Agatha Kakos."

"Me." She raised a hand, the disappointment in her voice as clear as the glass windows behind her.

Women take their revenge at the time of the affront; afterward is too late. Then you're already a victim. Her mother's pearl of wisdom echoed in her mind.

"Sign here," he replied, thrusting forward the handheld and a small plastic stylus.

She dragged the rubber tip along the screen, her name becoming blurry, tears threatening anew. It took every bit of sanity she had left to summon the will to keep those tears back.

The delivery driver shoved the envelope toward her and she numbly locked her hand around it. "Thank you, ma'am, and have a wonderful evening."

Her response involved slamming the door and slumping against it, letting a sob escape, followed by a wailing moan. He'd never be back. She'd never get a chance to take back the part of her he destroyed. And deep in her heart, the whispers of how she did this to herself, the thought of starting over again, of being alone, swallowed her whole.

The envelope was clutched in her hands, a tangible

chance to take her mind off reality. She ripped into it, pulling out a single piece of paper. It smelled like coffee, salt, and spring air. The words drew her eyes. An invitation...

An admirer seeks a muse.

Come, sip a cold beverage, taste the Mediterranean, and be inspired at Cupid's Cafe.

No special attire is required. Come as you are two days from now at noon. Our establishment sits on the corner of Bardstown Road and Eastern. A once-in-a-lifetime, second-chance date you won't want to miss.

Sincerely, Mr. Heart

Maybe there was hope for her after all.

MURPHY O'SHEA SAID goodbye to the friendly neighborhood police officers with the promise of following up with them if he remembered anything else. Coming home from grocery shopping to find his apartment broken into hadn't been the part hurting him the most. Living not far from Louisville's East District, closer to the bar district known as Highlands, break-ins happened quite frequently. No, what killed him—finding almost all his paintings destroyed. The same paintings scheduled to be transported to his friend's gallery the next day in preparation for his upcoming show.

Each canvas possessed a bit of his soul; they'd been beautiful pieces displaying his love for color and the tedious technique of tempura. Very few modern artists practiced his method, which required a lot of eggs. In fact, he'd been buying more eggs for his art when this mess occurred. The police noted the smashed door, recommended he install a security system, and inquired if he had any threats or enemies.

Ha! Funny. He had nothing of the sort. No one knew him outside of his renters, therapist, therapy group, and a few friends. And even if enemies existed, his work had consumed him these past few months. Nothing exciting happened outside of painting. Days had passed when he wouldn't even check the mail or leave his studio room.

He'd been thankful for the few friends he had making sure he ate and keeping him sane because his troubles ran beyond painter's tunnel vision. Even now, the miniature replicas of famous statues on his fireplace mantel no longer occupied their usual spots. No burglar would do something so silly, and fear gripped him that maybe his illness was progressing into a more severe form.

The cell phone in his pocket vibrated, blasting out Drowning Pool's "Bodies." A ringtone specifically selected for his friend, Patrick, who went through girls like people used paper plates. He answered and let out a sad and pitiful, "Hi."

"I called as soon as I got your message. Talk to me, Murphy."

"They're gone. All of them. Months of work destroyed in senseless destruction." He ran a hand through his blond hair, tugging on the tips. It had grown out in the last couple months. Preparing for his first show left no time for a haircut.

"Is everyone else okay? Trix and the kid?" Surprisingly, his friend held a note of concern in his voice for his renters. *A sense of humanity, surprising.*

Murph kicked at the edge of one of the ruined canvases, doing his best to lock down the scream he wanted to let out. "The other building was left untouched. I'm the lucky winner of having my life ruined."

"Buddy, I've heard these depressing words before, dark shit and dangerous. Maybe you should take your pills."

"They don't work like some magic thing to clear away the bad stuff. Never have. Consistency is what makes the damn things successful, and I've been cold turkey too long." Plus, if there were mythical drugs to keep him sane, he'd already be on them. Funny how even those closest to him didn't understand how this stuff worked. Sympathy was one thing they offered, but actual understanding proved a completely different story. "I can't do the show, Patrick."

"You need to find a way, friend. It's too late to turn back. I've got my rep on the line." They'd met on a fluke accident with him walking into Patrick's gallery to take a closer look at a couple paintings. He never expected the gallery owner to actively quiz him on his painting knowledge nor invite him to bring back his work at another time, which he'd done about a week later. Since then they'd become friends and partners, investing in his art and working toward his first show, a show he couldn't pull off anymore.

"And you always say I'm the dramatic one."

"No dramatics about it. Your display photo has gained interest. A serious tempera buyer, he's throwing out words like 'leading edge contemporary' and 'revivalist.' So, the show must go on."

Murph sighed, fingers stretching out, grabbing the statue of David and putting it on the right end of the mantel. Back where it belonged. "How the hell do you expect that to happen?"

"Don't get lost, first of all. Just focus. We already have five completed pieces at the gallery. You need twelve more and then leave the rest to me."

Twelve more, and creating the last nine had been more challenging than pulling teeth. His muse was gone, disappeared from his life, and he'd spent months reaching, draining every ounce of her from his mind and body, pouring it through his fingertips. A steady knock came on the screen door frame.

"Let me think about it, Rick. Someone's at the door. I got to go." He moved away from the fireplace, hoping the visitor wasn't Trix or another nosy neighbor worried about the police presence.

His buddy growled at the use of the nickname Murph called him. He hated nicknames. "If you don't say yes, I'll bother you until you do. Your personal fucking shadow, and if you really do drop, you lose out. No do-overs. It's now or never."

Those words had him longing to drag this out, to make someone else experience a twinge of the anxiety he experienced at those words. So, he hung up without any preamble, a press of a button and the angry tones disappeared. He slid the phone into his coat pocket and opened the door, ready to rehash his conversation with the cops for the concerned citizen. Instead, he got the following from a short, pudgy UPS courier, "Are you Mr. Murphy O'Shea?"

"Yes."

"Sign here, please."

So he did, giving his signature scrawl of his first and last name before being handed an envelope with no return address except a stamp from Cupid's Cafe. He'd never heard of the place, nor had he ordered anything so small. No canvases would be delivered until the next day.

He shut the screen, locked it, and walked into his living room to sit on the couch. The place looked like a damn mess. All his paintings strewn across the wood floor, cut and ripped, some defiled with markers. Fucking devastating, the helplessness caused him to slouch, almost folding in on himself, inside and out. Motivation all but destroyed, he saw no way to replace all the work from the last few months.

Looking at the envelope, he'd half a mind to throw it away, but a voice whispered inside him to take a peek. A lack of good news, no harm and no foul, this day ended with enough bad crap and all his work being ruined took the cake. So, he pulled out the letter. The letter proved to be an invitation, which said:

AN ADMIRER LOOKS FORWARD to meeting with you.

It's been a while since you spoke, but they haven't forgotten. Come, sip a cold beverage, taste the Mediterranean, and reminisce at Cupid's Cafe.

No special attire is required. Come as you are two days from now at noon. Our establishment sits on the corner of Bardstown Road and Eastern. A once-in-a-lifetime, second-chance date you won't want to miss.

Sincerely, Mr. Heart

MURPH LAUGHED, a sick, halfhearted sound coming out of his mouth with little effort. Who could he possibly know that would want to catch up? An admirer? Only one person came to mind at the word, and she'd disappeared a few years prior. Then again, why the hell not? This might be a gift or a new muse to inspire him, and he'd need all the inspiration possible to produce twelve paintings in two months. He got up and stuck the letter to his refrigerator before opening the door to grab water.

"Murph?" Trix's voice called through the screen door, echoing off the foyer and into his apartment. "What happened to the front door?"

He sighed. There'd been a moment where he thought

visitors wouldn't show up. Where he'd have a silent evening in which he'd get away without having to explain the break-in to anyone until tomorrow.

"Give me a minute. Be right there."

Praying silently, he hoped the date in a couple days would be a ray of sunshine in his world of cloudy skies.

Chapter Two

Aggie stepped up on the corner sidewalk and glanced up. The sign for Cupid's Cafe jutted out from the building on a metal rack, lit up in hues of blue and cream. The windows were clear with white shutters on either side capable of being shut at closing time. From her position outside, she could tell sheer panels hung from the ceilings, draped between pillars. The place wasn't crowded but contained a fair amount of patrons, and she took a step forward, working up the courage to go inside.

Her viewings with potential apartments turned into a big bust and she'd taken the day off, shuffling her clients around and re-arranging appointments by trading a few folks with another nutritionist. Something she'd most likely regret later, but she needed extra time to search for an apartment and work up to the meeting with her admirer scheduled to happen in minutes.

Admirer. The word gave her goose bumps and did strange things to her stomach. Would, could this be Jordan? Or some man she'd never met who stalked her?

There were too many possibilities and thinking of them made her gut churn like a smoothie blender.

Before she could get any closer, the front door to the cafe opened, and there stood a tall, gorgeous man in a three-piece suit, collar open. His face reflected Nordic qualities, blond hair, light blue eyes, and an angular nose. Those eyes, in particular, pierced her, honed her focus and then he beckoned her to him.

"Agatha?" he asked, extending his hand out, waiting for hers. Was he her admirer? She'd never seen him before.

She placed her hand in his extremely warm one. "Aggie. And you are?"

"Angel, I manage the cafe. We were expecting you. Come inside and let me guide you." The smile he gave revealed perfect teeth, and for a fraction of a second, she got a little disappointed. A gorgeous man like this deserved a date as much as she did.

Following his lead, she stepped through the door, and her mood shifted. Before entering, awkwardness bubbled up within her, a typical reaction she experienced toward social situations. Now, a wave of calm washed over her, relaxing her muscles, and the room possessed the perfect ambient temperature.

People sat on couches, around tall tables, and in small booths absorbed in conversation, trading smiles and laughs. The patrons didn't even seem to notice her and she was gifted with disregard instead of typical curious or pity-filled gazes. Music played in the background, harp and guitar mingling with one another. The scent of coffee and bread blended in the air, and maybe a hint of chocolate. Angel tugged gently on her coat sleeve, directing her farther into the cafe.

"We serve a variety of beverages, from alcohol to any

coffee, house treat. There's also food selections, including barbecue lamb bites. I highly recommend."

"Sounds delicious," she murmured, still glancing around at her surroundings. The small stage in the corner sat bare for the moment but was equipped with a stool and microphone for the budding poet or musician. An area separate from the tables and booths was filled with bean bags and a small group of folks sat cross-legged on several, smoking from a hookah.

"Yes, they are and here is the bar. Order whatever you like."

She looked past the manager to the wooden bar decorated with the faces and bodies of mermaids similar to the ones seen on the bows of ships. A man leaned against the counter at the far end. His ash blond hair, a bit longer than Jordan's black locks. He wore a faded-green long-sleeved coat, jeans, and a pair of boots.

Angel pointed at the barista conversing with the man and snapped his fingers. "Thalia will help you." The barista smiled and drew her hand down the patron's arm before ending the connection abruptly, a helpful, flirty woman. "Help this young lady with her selection, please."

"What will let go of your inhibitions?" Thalia asked with a saucy half-grin and only then did her previous customer turn to glance at Aggie.

His face she remembered, but couldn't quite place. Though the smile that lit his features told her they'd met before.

"I'll have an Americano, please," Aggie replied.

"Agatha?" The voice did it, throwing her back to two years prior and her therapy group. It was the tall, skinny dude with the face scruff, whom she'd always thought attractive, but kept things polite because of where they'd been. He was clean shaven now, with grey starting to come in at his temples, making his blond hair appear lighter.

"Murphy O'Shea, right?"

His grin grew wider and the barista appeared forgotten as he twisted his body to face her. "You remember."

"I did when you spoke. You look different without the facial hair."

A chuckle burst from him. "I can't believe you remember my poor attempt at a beard, too. I gave up trying to grow it out. A lost cause and it made me look a little too hipster. So, what brings you here?"

Interesting question and she waffled between lying and telling the truth. Would she look desperate to be seeking an admirer in a random coffeehouse café? Then she decided to go with her gut. "Received an invitation to meet an admirer. I got it a couple days ago."

For a moment, he didn't say anything, and Thalia appeared again with her order. "One Americano."

"What do I owe you?"

The gal shook her head, black curls bouncing in the air. "Nothing. It's on the house, courtesy of Mr. Heart. May you two enjoy your chance to reconnect."

Aggie stepped up and grabbed the paper coffee cup. A pair of hearts entwined on the side caught her eye as a warm cup met her cold hands.

"Well, I guess I should confess to getting a letter, too."

"You did?" She pivoted her body to lean against the bar, enjoying the idea she wasn't alone. Showing up here hadn't been a lost cause. "You admire me?"

His cheeks went a little pink. She'd made him blush. *How adorable.*

He cleared his throat. "Yes...uh, I did. I mean, I do admire you. In group, you always played cheerleader for the rest of us and provided a good example." Another pause as he took a gulp of his own drink. Then, "Want to grab a table?"

"Yes." She might have responded too quickly or been a bit eager, but if he noticed then he acted the perfect gentleman by not commenting. No, his reaction was to slide off the too-tall bar seat and head toward a booth against the cafe window. They could watch passersby or focus on each other.

When he slid into one side, she sat opposite. "This is perfect."

"You think so?" He sounded genuinely concerned about her opinion, glancing anywhere but at her. Murph always came off a little insecure in the group and from his action, the insecurities were still present.

So, she reached out and let her fingertips touch the back of his hand. A spark occurred. The warmth of his hand tingling through the connection made her want to latch on and link their fingertips. A strange sensation since she'd never experienced a lot of personal displays of affection or closeness growing up. No, her mother didn't believe touching an essential part of daily interactions.

Murph's focus went to their point of joining.

"The booth is great. Don't doubt your decision." She gave a soft, no teeth smile aimed to inspire good energy. The effort and her reaction to him made her realize she trusted him on a small level, even when she rarely trusted anyone with anything. Jordan was a perfect example of why she shouldn't.

"Thanks. You always know how to lift my ego."

Egos. She'd had enough of guys super inflated by them. This man never showed such signs.

"Well, yours is a lot smaller than the ones I've dealt with." The bitterness in her voice crept in again, as it seemed to do with more frequency since her break-up, and she found it difficult to hide those emotions.

"Speaking from experience?"

"A bad breakup, and my ex owned a huge ego."

"Is this the same guy you started dating right before you left the group?"

Yes, a stupid mistake. She'd believed Jordan could be as therapeutic as a whole circle of folks discussing their problems and lifting each other.

She nodded in response. "I'd love to say I woke up one morning and figured out I needed to move on, but not the case in this particular situation."

She'd remember this moment for a while when Murph encased her hand with his. A reverse hand grasp, increasing the amount of contact and she relaxed into it, his comfort. Normally, she'd have pulled away, a knee jerk reaction to being embraced. But in this instance she wanted the offering Murph gave her, similar to what he'd done for her in group before. This wasn't the first time he'd been a comfort to her.

When she flexed her hand within his, he flexed back. "Sorry this guy acted like such a douche."

"You have no idea."

"Tell me," he replied after taking a quick sip of his drink with his free hand. She finally took a pull of hers, loving the taste of semi-hot coffee, dark and deep, working its way down her throat. The beverage acting as a soothing, welcome taste in her mouth before she let loose the ugly, nasty of her once-upon-a-time.

"Sure you're up to it?" No sense in putting someone else through her hell. Especially when this failed to make her list of planned conversation. No, she'd rather bottle up her ex's memory and toss him in the Ohio River.

He shook his head. "With my issues, I'm never up for

anything, but if there's one thing I learned in group, it was how to be a good listener. Lay it on me."

She inhaled deeply and on the exhale, let the words pour out. "We dated for the last two years. At first, he acted like a dream come true—attentive, caring, kind, and so good at helping me work through my problems. He also took his time, no rushing things, which without dragging this out longer, is huge for me. Then we made plans this year to move in together.

"We found a duplex, put down a down payment, and I turned in my notice at my current place. Right after, he started to grow distant, cancelling plans because of work...all this insane stuff, the complete opposite of the man I'd come to know."

She paused, taking a break to gulp a big swallow of coffee. As if the beverage would stave off the moisture starting to pool in her eyes. Crying never played a big role in her life. At least, she kept the tears private when she experienced the urge to let them out.

"A couple weeks ago, he told me he needed a break, which I...it was fine. I can imagine it's a bit nerve-wracking to move in with someone when you're used to being on your own." The first tear leaked out, trailing a path down her cheek. Near the bursting point, the urge to yell in frustration at her weakness seemed acute. *Strong women never cry*. "But when I went over a few days ago to talk...to discuss where we were heading, another woman answered the door."

A second tear escaped from the other eye and Murph reached out to make contact. One finger to her tear. A secondary spark, the connection she wanted to hold on to. *Grab his hand and put it against my cheek. Steal his warmth.* Rogue, dumb thoughts, the exact opposite of what a strong woman needed.

"Sorry." He gave a sheepish smile, almost a guilty one. He pulled back, disconnecting from her, taking his hands away.

"What for?"

"I didn't ask permission. The second time I've put my hands on you today, and all I can say is sorry. I'm a bit impulsive sometimes." Another thing to find attractive about him: his polite and gentlemanly attitude, which other men of her acquaintance—including her ex—failed to possess at all times. She'd never seen Murph without it.

She laughed at the awkwardness of the situation and how comfortable his touch made things; it wasn't the first time she found herself thankful for him. "Would you think it weird if I said I'm okay with it?"

Her answer surprised him by his dropped jaw and then the quick scratch to said jaw, but without the scruff of yesteryear, the movement looked clumsy. "No, not at all. So, where does this whole thing leave you?"

"Hunting for an apartment, at least somewhere else to live, since I already turned in my notice at my current place, and it's not like I'm getting the duplex from Jordan. We put everything in his name, much to my regret."

They both went silent and the noise of the room intruded. Murph looked thoughtful, and she reached up to wipe her lips, then tucked loose strands of hair behind each ear. Here she sat, telling everything to someone she'd known years ago in a therapy group, one she'd only been in as a way to help enforce her commitment to not binge. He probably thought she let some cats loose near a bowl of cucumbers.

"I'm going to head to the ladies' room for a minute."

"Sounds good. Want a refill?" He pointed at her empty coffee cup.

Aggie shook her head. "No, that's all right."

Pushing back her chair, she stood and left, feeling his eyes watch her go. A small part of her wanted to glance back like the high school girl she'd once been checking to see if the boy she admired looked her way. But she schooled herself and kept on moving without turning her head. Strong women survived this way, by never showing weakness. After the tears she'd shed, she needed to regain strength.

MURPHY WATCHED HER WALK AWAY. The sway of her hips, the sweetheart shape of her ass, and the way her jeans hugged those curves. He'd dreamt about them. Not only them but the woman herself and her smile. A smile she no longer allowed to reach her eyes. She'd once radiated hope and optimism.

Such high spirits raised the entire group, and they fed off the energy. Those emotions got him through many days when the world seemed too dark to keep on going. Now, the irony of running into her, the one woman who helped him stage a comeback she'd no idea of. And already new images, new inspiration came to him.

He could paint her right there, across from him in this very booth, with two tears, each trailing a path of woe down her creamy skin. The skin he'd always imagined as soft, and with his muse right in front of him, he'd reached out and touched the smooth expanse of her hand. Silky another adjective he'd use to describe those hands.

Damn. He shouldn't have acted so impulsively. Nope, his touch hurt everything, but canvas and paint.

Signaling the barista behind the counter, he asked for a couple glasses of water. She gave him a wink in response and returned with the glasses as Aggie slipped into her seat.

"What's this for?" she asked, sweeping her hair over her shoulder. The black tresses featured in some of his daydreams as well.

"I was thirsty for water, so I figured I wouldn't be rude and at least get you one, too."

Her smile came back, more genuine than the ones from earlier, the mood lightening once more. "You're too sweet. So enough about my sad story. Tell me all about you. What's life been like over the last two years?"

It'd be easy to bring up the struggle, the daily battles, and the two hospital stints when the medicine failed to work, but who wanted to hear about more sad things? At the same time, his latest troubles involved sadness as well.

"I've been working toward my first show."

"Show? Like theater?"

He wouldn't blame her for not remembering. They'd only talked about his painting once. The day he really noticed her and started paying attention to the words, the stories she shared with the group. When he'd mentioned how the light reflected off her hair, casting her in an angelic glow. "Painting. I'm a tempera painter, and finally, after too many years to count, I have a show coming up."

"Yes, that's right. You're a starving artist. I remember you discussing this a little bit during group, but what is tempera?"

"Tempera painting is like creating art with quick-drying paint, that's the easiest way to describe it, and the process is lengthier than other mediums like oils or water-based colors."

"The whole thing sounds fascinating. When is the show?"

He grinned at the idea she remembered his passion.

"In about twelve weeks. Only hiccup is all my paintings were destroyed last night."

The joy in her face fell away, and he found himself thankful for another person to share in his woes. Patrick and Trix, they tried, but couldn't understand.

"Absolutely heartbreaking, what happened?"

"Someone broke in, but I'm getting a security company to install a system. No more risk taking here." He winked, hoping to give her confidence in him, in his coping skills, even if they were virtually non-existent outside of this one step. "That's what I was doing before coming here, talking to a security company."

"Sounds a lot more interesting than apartment hunting. Can you recover the paintings?"

"No, they're destroyed. I have to paint new ones. Twelve to be exact."

She took a drink of the water. "Sounds like a lot of work."

"It will be." When had the conversation become stilted again? They were going through the motions, playing a game of general conversation. "Would it be weird if I offered you an apartment at my complex? I know we've never talked about it, but I own two buildings, two apartments in each. I've got one open right now. Rent would be minimal. A great way to get out of the place with all the memories and give you time to save up. Housing isn't cheap anywhere in this town anymore."

She laughed, a low sound sending a bolt of desire straight to his groin. "You're sweet, just like the water, but I could be a serial killer."

"If you are, then you're the prettiest one I've ever met." He doubted she could hurt a butterfly. No, this woman wouldn't harm anyone, not with what she'd been through.

Silence reigned once more and she raised an eyebrow

at him. He snorted, realizing the joke was crap. "I guess it's a pretty morbid pick-up line."

Aggie shook her head and chuckled. "Yep, I'd look for new material."

Her reaction dispelled the insanity, but didn't obliterate the fear that he'd never get to see her after today. He wanted to see her again.

"I'll add 'search for new pick-up lines' to my to-do list along with my twelve paintings and paying the bills." He grabbed the extra napkin on the table, a white paper with Cupid's Cafe in a beautiful script, then reached into his pocket for the pen he always carried.

Ideas sometimes came to him at a moment's notice and he'd draw sketches with anything he could find, even his own skin became a canvas for the initial idea. Instead of drawing, like he wanted to do, he wrote his number on the paper, traced over it twice to make it easy to read, and the black ink bled into the soft paper, inking its permanent way to the sheet. "So, before I forget, here's my number. You won't let me give you a place to sleep, at least take this so if you ever want to talk."

"Do you still go to group?"

He shook his head, but he kept silent on the subject. Better left for another day. "No, I stopped over a year ago."

"Oh." Her single word spoke volumes. Maybe she planned to go back; he'd do the same if it meant he could see her.

"But if you want an intro back into the group, a friendly face to go with you—"

"No, not at all. I don't think group is for me anymore, but thanks." She glanced at her phone, a sure sign their date would come to an end. He noticed the napkin with his number still sat there, hovering between them and ominous. Would she take it?

Please. He prayed silently in his head the same word, over and over, along with the physical thought she'd grab the napkin and stuff it in her pocket.

Aggie reached for it, folded it neatly and stuck it in her coat pocket. He held fast to the intense urge to whoop for joy and also to stay calm. Insane how one gesture inspired the manic part of him. Then the elation ebbed and relief rushed in. Now would be the worst time to experience an episode.

"I understand completely. Sometimes you need to move on, and things. Damn, I'm not good at small talk."

"I think you did great, Murphy. Let's do this again sometime, okay?"

He grinned. "Yes, let's. When?"

"I'll call you." She slid out of the booth and he followed suit. He'd forgotten the protocol—handshake or hug? Not wanting to bungle things or appear creepy, he settled for extending his hand, and then she surprised him again, throwing her arms around his shoulders and giving him a brief squeeze.

"I think we're beyond handshakes at this point," she said once she pulled back.

The sweet smell of her shampoo or perfume, a coconut scent, still lingered in his nostrils, paired with all the moments of their time today, would carry his muse for a while. "Good to know."

Her response was a shake of a head, a laugh, and then a quick, "I'll call you."

He stood there for minutes after she'd walked away and out the door. Until, finally, he went his own way. He waited so he wouldn't be tempted to run after her, to invite her to dinner, or anything else. No, he'd settle for a quick grocery store stop for more eggs. It'd be a long night.

Chapter Three

From the moment Murph set foot in the door, he'd been working. First the background, all gray and dim, much like his life. Then he started on the sketch of Aggie. Giving form to her standing in the doorway, right before she'd left the cafe. The moment freeze-framed in his mind, a perfect reflection of her sadness.

She wouldn't have admitted to it, of course. Yet, her eyes gave it away. Weeping without tears. Her hair came easiest, a beacon to him that mixed perfect with her naturally olive skin. She was amazing and didn't know it, and that's how he painted her, beauty shining bright, but her face and posture completely oblivious to the fact. So different.

A knock came at his front door, and he hollered, "Come in."

"If you don't want people breaking into your house, you shouldn't leave the front door unlocked." Trix approached him and put a hand on his shoulder.

He set his painting plate down and looked at her hand on him. Nothing. Murph tried to feel more than friendship for the woman who showed up to take care of him all the time, but no luck. He pulled away from her and pointed at the painting.

"Is this new?" She stepped up to the picture, eyes wide.

"Yes. I've begun working on it today."

A frown marred her narrow, freckled face, "All day?"

"Since I got back this afternoon. What time is it?" He purposely kept this room clock-free. Art needed to be given free rein. When the lighting from the sun disappeared, he turned on the track lighting, positioned perfectly to illuminate his workspace.

"One in the morning." She faced him now, eyes filled with concern and maybe even pity. "I came over because your lights were still on and it's so late. Have you eaten?"

"I grabbed a jug of tea and a sandwich a while ago."

"You don't know what time, do you?" Her question was simple, straight forward, but regardless, it reminded him of his inability to keep up with the smallest things. Becoming absorbed in something seemed to be the worst; according to his previous therapist, it wasn't ideal for someone with his condition.

Hours passed, half of a day—no big deal to him. He'd keep working until the job was complete. In a way, he believed it kept him from hitting a depressive mood, but some people and the therapist believed he exhibited borderline manic behavior.

"It was shortly after I got back before the sun went down. But I'm not hungry, I may turn in for the night."

She walked up to him, placing her hand, thin with long, spindly fingers on his cheek in a caress. "I can make some eggs or something real quick. Seth is already asleep, and it won't take me long."

The reminder her six-year-old son slept next door

swamped him with guilt. How many times had she put her child's safety at risk to bother with him?

"No, don't worry about it. With the break-in, it's better if you don't leave him alone. The security systems will be installed tomorrow, and then everything will be good."

"You're always taking such good care of us." Leaning up on her tiptoes, she pressed her lips against his. The tips of her blond, blue-streaked hair brushed against his arm. Her eyes closed, but his didn't. He kept them open and desire failed to stir. No, all parts of him that should have reacted remained dormant.

When she broke the connection and stepped back, moisture filled her eyes.

"Trix—I'm sorry. I...we're better off as friends."

Her lips thinned and eyes narrowed as she pointed at the picture of Aggie. "Is it because of her?"

"No, she's unattainable. It's because I'm not what you need. You need someone to take care of you, not the opposite. I already take up too much of your time, take you away from Seth."

"Not true." She approached him again and this time hugged him. "You take care of me. This place...your belongings. You forget things, not an issue, and I told you before that Seth loves you, too. He understands when I need to help."

Murph let out a sigh and pried Tricia's arms from around him. The nickname Trix, something he called her because of her ever changing hair color, but for some reason, the moment brought her real name to the forefront of his mind. They needed to be more formal about things, if anything, to get his point across. A relationship, beyond friendship, between them wasn't possible, due to his lack of attraction and because he'd known her most of his life.

"That may be the case, but I can never give you everything." Holding onto her arms, he moved her away from his body, forcing her to look at him in the eyes. "I'm broken, Tricia."

"I'm not asking for everything." She smiled and pecked his cheek with those same lips. "I'll make you those eggs now and some toast. Soup's on in ten minutes."

Then she moved off to his kitchen like their conversation never happened. He'd made his thoughts known so he wouldn't force her out. The last thing she needed from him was a firm voice of censure, especially since he rejected her. Maybe cooking acted as her way of coping, like painting was for him. So, he'd let her cook. Yet, the damage was done, concentration broken, and his work on this portrait halted for the night.

* * *

THE DAY before had been a whirlwind. Truthfully, Aggie never expected to run into always-quiet-sexy-as-sin-Murph, and she'd been rather surprised at how easy it was to talk to him, to touch him. Yes, talking with someone who would refrain from judging her or her feelings was something she'd missed.

They'd learned the practice in group; voices deserved to be heard without censor. A connection had formed between them as they'd talked, held hands, though they beat around the bush a bit. She expected him to invite her out for dinner or something, but when he kept quiet, she went home, alone.

It had been hard not to dig into the sweets still sitting on the coffee table from her previous fall-from-the-wagon. Instead, she'd settled for a romantic comedy marathon and a salad, reminding herself someone...a male someone, liked her and admired her.

Now, she lay in bed on a Saturday and attempted to find the motivation to move. The phone rang as she began to contemplate sleeping a few more hours. She wondered if it was Murph before remembering they hadn't exchanged numbers. No, she'd been given a number but not asked for one in return.

"Hello."

Mrs. Sanders voice greeted her. "Aggie? Hope I didn't wake you."

"No, I'm awake." A state she'd rather not be.

"I know we talked the other day about you staying on month-to-month..." Her landlady paused and a hard knot formed in Aggie's stomach.

"Yes?"

"Well, the thing is, my daughter got a job transfer from St. Louis to Louisville. It's all rather sudden, but she needs a place to stay, and I need to give her your apartment."

Her body went stiff and she tried to keep herself calm. Strong women stayed calm in tough situations. "How long do I have?"

She'd known this was a possibility. There was always a chance, and to be honest, there was no legal obligation owed to her, not with her lease fulfilled and the landlord not offering a renewal.

"By next weekend, dear. My daughter is flying in two weeks and if you're out, she can move my grandbaby and her husband in shortly after. Sorry this is so sudden."

"It's okay. I understand." She really didn't, but respecting her elders had been drilled into her from a young age and really these things happened to her. Getting worked up wouldn't do any good except make her upset. Being upset led to binge eating, and binge eating only got her on her knees praying to the porcelain god. A strong woman channeled this bump in the road into a chance for a new opportunity, even with nausea swamping her stomach.

"Thank you. My daughter is happy to be coming back home, and I'll admit I'll like having her and the baby nearby. It's been almost a year since I've seen them."

"Oh, well this will be good, then. Mrs. Sanders, I have to go...need to start apartment hunting." Truth trumped all the lies of fake happiness she wanted to tell, but regardless, she had to get off the phone. Now.

"Have a nice day, dear. And good luck."

She hung up without a goodbye and then rolled over, screaming into her pillow. Yep, no strong woman lived here.

Why me? Why this? "Why did you have to break up with me, Jordan?" He wasn't there to respond, but it needed to be said. If he'd stuck to the plan and not turned into an asshole, she'd be safe in their duplex right now, curled up in his king-sized bed.

The reality of the situation was she had no place to live in a week, and no money to get a new place if she did. Her entire savings she'd turned over to her ex to pay the down payment on their duplex. A mistake to remind her about trusting people with everything.

Then she remembered Murphy and his crazy suggestion. Her mind did a quick tally in her head. If she negotiated a deal for minimum rent, she'd have enough saved in two months for a place. It'd be weird trying to rely on someone she barely knew...hell, after the Jordan incident, relying on anyone sounded like a bad joke. Forcing her body to get up came with little struggle, motivated out of desperation to keep a roof over her head. She grabbed the napkin from her coat and dialed the number.

Each ring added to the boulder in her stomach. Each

round adding to the possibility of rejection that she'd be living out of her car in seven days. Then..."Hello?"

"Murphy?"

"Aggie?"

She laughed. "Good morning. I'm surprised you know my voice." In fact, he continued to surprise her.

"It's a hard one to forget. What can I do for you?"

Give me a place to live. Instead, "Just wanted to see how you were doing," came out.

"Good. I stayed up late painting but got a few hours of shut-eye. I'm getting ready to get going again."

"Oh, I don't want to bother you. If I am, I can talk to you later." She tried to sound like everything was fine, putting on her best nonchalant voice.

He scoffed. "Who said that? A friend calling me is more interesting than painting, at the moment. Are you sure you're okay?"

Obviously, her casual voice sucked. "I'm good but… were you serious about offering me a place to live yesterday?"

"I said it, so I meant it. What's up?"

He'd already asked her the same thing three times, so she got to it.

"My landlord, she's kicking me out." The words sounded harsher than she'd meant. *Damn*.

"What bullshit."

"It's not too crazy. I'm on a month-to-month, no lease, and was supposed to be out a few weeks ago. Until the Jordan thing. Her daughter's moving into town and needs a place...anyways, I've got to get out by next week." She'd rattled off the story so fast, she doubted he'd heard half of it.

Yet, he still responded quickly. "Then my spare place is yours. Free of charge."

Alarm bells sounded in her head. Free of charge usually meant at some point she'd get on someone's nerves. Her mother's own non-employment, her father leaving, and the subsequent stepfather's she'd had taught her riding free was never a good idea. Nope, she needed a place for two months and would negotiate.

"I appreciate the offer, but I can't allow myself to take advantage of you. It's not good business sense, especially since you're working on your paintings for the show. Let me pay you something, at least, to cover utilities and a base room charge in case you have to do any cleaning after I'm gone for the next tenant."

"I can't take advantage of a friend in hard place. That wouldn't be right."

She sighed. "I understand, but I feel the same way. We're both in tough places right now."

Murph had gone silent and for a moment, she wondered if he'd changed his mind. It'd be her luck. Instead, he shocked her again.

"How about you come and see the apartment before we strike a bargain? You may not want to stay here after you see it."

Unbelievable. "You make it sound like a run-down place with rats and cockroaches."

He chuckled, a low, deep sound that sent a tingle down her spine. She stood there in her PJs with goose bumps thanks to him. "I haven't seen any, but you never know."

"All right, what time?"

"Today, anytime. Is this your cell number?"

"Yes."

"I'll text you the address, and you swing by at your leisure."

She smiled at his openness and casual ways. "What if my leisure is midnight?"

"I'll probably be up."

Completely disarming, the best way to describe him, and he acted so free when she believed in being the exact opposite.

"Sounds good. I'll come by this afternoon."

"Like I said, whenever." The attitude made her nervous, and a little daring. It had been two years since she'd gone to another guy's apartment, though this was a bit different.

"Okay. Bye, Murph."

"Bye, Aggie." His voice sounded soft as he said her name, sparking another shiver. Why did this feel like so much more than seeing an apartment? No clue, but she needed to refrain from it becoming more. She needed stability, and such a thing came from keeping herself professional and aloof. Not by getting involved with a potential landlord. Straight and narrow, strong women followed that path, unlike her mother's idea of strong women aligning themselves with a man.

Chapter Four

Murph had barely been able to concentrate since his phone call with Aggie. He rapid-fire cleaned the upstairs apartment and organized all his painting supplies. The main living/dining area had served as his studio for the last year or so. He'd need to get everything moved out and maybe a fresh paint job. There'd be a ton of things to do if she agreed to move in.

If being the key word in the sentence. She'd possibly see the place and run away screaming. The apartments were old, though, his friend Patrick called them ancient. He'd failed to update the style or the design inside and out, choosing to leave things the way his grandmother had for memories and money's sake.

His mind started wandering to thoughts of his nana, and then the doorbell rang. Scrambling down the stairs, he stopped himself from running into the wall next to the door. Breath check, run a hand through the hair, and a quick face pat to ensure his typical two-day-old scruff wasn't out of control.

Then he opened the door. She faced away from him

and when she turned the action played out in slow motion, from the swish of her hair to her smile. Everything became better. The frantic moments of before gone in a flash.

"Hi." His greeting came out a little breathless, and if anything, it made her smile bigger.

"Hi, I found it."

He opened the screen door, stepping to the side to let her walk in. "You did, though it's kind of hard to miss."

The buildings were a tangerine-colored brick, which dulled and cracked over the years thanks to the awesome Louisville winters.

"Makes it easier to find. Also, it's unique. These buildings don't match anything else around here. It's got a vintage vibe," Aggie said as she stepped across the threshold and looked around.

The screen door creaked shut, and then they stood in front of each other. There were so many things he needed to say, and instead, he picked the first thing that came to mind. "How do you do that?"

"What?" She twirled with a chunk of her hair, wrapping it around her finger. What he wouldn't give to be that hair.

"You take negative things and turn them positive. It's not something I'm very good at."

"I learned. Bad stuff happens, and you have to look at the ways those bad things can be good. Losing my place means the chance at a new experience, albeit, not at my usual pace. Is the apartment first floor or second?"

Thank goodness she'd started driving the conversation because he found himself a bit helpless, at the moment—a tongue-tied slave to his admiration of her. "Second floor, follow me."

As they started up the wooden staircase, he began extolling on the history. "This place was built in the nineteen-fifties. My grandmother bought this building and the one next door in the seventies and refurbished them into the apartments they are now. She basically made her income from this place and always kept at least one renter. I've got two in the other building, and I live in the downstairs apartment here."

The door was still open at the top of the stairs only a few steps off the landing. He walked in, hoping she followed. "There are two bedrooms, a bathroom, living area, and kitchen/dining area. There's also a small balcony if you like city sounds."

She came around him and started to explore. He liked her cautious manner. Found it adorable, like a cat in new surroundings with her quiet steps and peering head. "Will you need to keep all your supplies in one of the rooms?"

"No, I'll move everything downstairs to my secondary studio. I tend to work up here when the light is good, but divide my time between both places. No hardship, really."

"Everything is electric?" She looked at the stove, the microwave, dishwasher, and refrigerator.

"No, the stove is gas. My grandmother kept it so all residents would have a way to cook if winter weather got bad. I saw no reason to change it."

He watched her wander through the living room, moving around his things and running her hand along the fireplace mantle as she looked around. The actions sparked a peaceful vein in him; he liked her here.

"The floors are natural wood. You can have rugs if you're worried about cold feet. Also, the fireplace works, and I have extra wood at the back of the building you're free to use."

"It is fall, isn't it?"

He laughed, "Well, it's just starting, but yes. Don't worry. I'm not good at keeping up with the seasons, either.

Trix...my neighbor has had to come over and convince me to light a fire dozens of times."

"Is painting a real distracting profession?"

He winked at her. "You have no idea."

Aggie stood there for a minute, unmoving and quiet. The awkward silence they'd shared before filling up space again.

"So, are you interested in the place?" He wanted to see her smile again, to be as comfortable with him as she'd been in the café.

"I am."

"Then let's hash out the details over coffee at my place." Damn, he sounded like a creeper. "I mean, would you like a cup of coffee?"

"Lead the way."

So he did, heading downstairs and into his apartment. Then he realized he hadn't cleaned up in here. No, his focus had been firmly on the rental. "I apologize for the mess."

Mess mainly meant the clothes strewn around the living room, the amassed coffee cups with half glasses of cold, curdled java. A few probably could've been submitted for local school science fairs. He heard her footsteps behind him, a little ways back, which provided enough time for him to scoop a pile of papers from one of the kitchen chairs and toss it on top of another pile on the counter.

"It's all right. I'm sure painting takes precedence over cleaning. As it should." There was a hesitance in her voice. Clearly doubt.

"Yes, and getting ready for this show has been the worst." He refused to look back at her. Censure was one thing capable of sending him in a spiral straight for hell. Instead, he kept busy with the coffee pot, rinsing out the re-usable filter, filling the pot with fresh water, measuring the grounds, and turning on the maker. Then the cups, cream, sugar, and stirrers...those little wooden ones Trix brought over. She'd seen them on sale.

He finally worked up the nerve to face her, realizing he'd let the conversation go as cold as those day old cups of coffee in the other room. She sat at the kitchen table. Not prying into his mail or touching the lazy Susan with his cow shakers. But the cow shakers were missing. He stepped forward reaching for the turner, spinning it clockwise. Eyes glued to all the pieces, the moon toothpick holder, and the cat fiddle bowl with various odds and ends, but no cow shakers. They were his grandmothers. Had he moved them?

"You didn't see a pair of cow salt and pepper shakers here by any chance?"

Aggie shook her head with a little side-eye. Sure, he sounded crazy, but if he'd moved things without remembering, it was a possible sign of delusions, something much worse than his regular symptoms. Maybe a new neighbor wasn't a good idea after all.

* * *

THE APARTMENT LOOKED GREAT, even if the neighborhood wasn't ideal. Aggie imagined her furniture in the space and could picture herself settled and relaxing in front of a blazing fire. The image pleasant and refreshing compared to the chaos of her life over the previous weeks. Then Murph invited her into his space. She'd never expected neat and tidy, but his place proved a bit messier than her imagining.

No judging at all, though. She refused to rate someone's worth based on how clean their house was, even if her mother always did. Though, he certainly appeared a bit guilty about the mess. Since the question about the shakers, he looked agitated, worried, by the downward tilt of his eyebrows and wrinkles in his forehead.

Then she noticed his eyes, not on her, but the roundabout in the center of the table, as if willing the shakers to appear. In group, they never shared their illnesses. Part of the whole no judgment deal. They talked about their challenges, but never really spelled out their problems. Aggie tried to recall Murph's story time and then let her words speak for her.

"The shakers, want to talk about them?" Best way to solve problems, at least, that's what they'd been taught in group. *Best way to reveal those needy parts of you.*

Nothing happened for another minute. Then he blinked. A good sign. "I had cow shakers. Right there, and now they're gone."

She knew she got messed up in social situations, rejection, or when insecurities, which, thanks to her mother's voice inside her head, was often, but something so small..."Maybe they are in the living room."

The smell of brewed coffee began to permeate the air and she inhaled deeply to calm herself. It'd be hard to live with him if things were always like this, not without becoming more involved. A strong woman worried about herself, took care of herself, not her too-cute-slightly-unstable-potential-landlord. "Do you think they are there?"

"What?" He looked at her, blinked twice, and really looked. Not a vacant expression and then he snapped out of it. "Damn, I'm sorry." Rubbing his eyes, he walked to the coffee pot. "I probably scared the shit out of you. Fuck. This shit I deal with."

A couple of brown mugs of steaming coffee later, he placed one in front of her and the sugar and creamer cows. The other shakers must have matched them. She doctored her coffee the way she liked it, two sugars and a splash of cream. Once she finished, Murph started in on turning his coffee into a sweet, creamed up frou-frou drink. His dirty blond hair lay in artful disarray, with his paint-stained khakis and a green T-shirt that said, "I don't want your Monet, honey." For being out of sorts, he looked horribly attractive.

"You like sugar and cream in your coffee?"

He stuck a stirrer in the cup and started to swirl everything. "Of course, I suffer from a psychiatric diagnosed disorder, but I'm not a masochist. Those who drink it black obviously like to torture themselves."

"Too true. So...you want to talk about what happened?" No sense in keeping it in. She hated holding things back, especially after the policy failed to work with her ex. Strong women confronted problems head on with protective armor in place.

"My problem? Surprise! Your potential landlord is bipolar, which manifests itself in impulse behaviors and fixations, with periodic depressive episodes, though those are less frequent. I'm very much a routine person. With the show, I've been breaking some of those routines and things have gone missing. It's a small setback, and hopefully, it will clear up itself."

No doubt lack of routine played a little havoc with his meds, most bi-polars she'd met preferred prescriptions to keep themselves under control, along with other treatment methods. She wanted to ask more questions: what prescription was he taking? How was his diet?

The nutritionist part of her, familiar with working with bi-polar and other mentally impaired patients, wanted to help. At the same time, it would've been rude to ask and went against the whole "Strong women—take care of yourself" mantra she wanted to maintain. "All right, I've heard worse things, and you're not a masochist, as you mentioned."

"Thank goodness. One strike in my favor, outside of my outburst, and again I apologize for scaring you. You're still interested in the place?"

"Definitely, but we have to work out some form of payment. I can't live here for free. It's not my style."

He nodded in agreement before taking a sip of his coffee. "I can respect that. What do you think is fair compensation?"

Humor radiated from his grey eyes. No doubt he knew how inappropriate the question sounded, and for a brief moment, the idea of them together entered her mind, kissing, touching and lying on her bed. She'd lie if anyone asked her if she found Murph attractive, since sleeping with a landlord fell into the "not wise" column.

"A couple hundred bucks a month and whatever utilities." She could stay professional and strong. Yes, she could, until she drank the coffee. A medium roast with a perfect mellow flavor, just the way she loved it. Waking up to a gorgeous man with coffee like this—

"Would you be offended if I said I don't want your money?"

Her immediate reaction was to blurt out yes, but she held back and thought about it. The hesitation led Murph to keep talking.

"Money's great, but I don't think I'd really be helping you. You need to save some cash, right?"

She nodded in agreement.

"Then let's figure out something else, and I have a suggestion not untoward."

Aggie giggled.

"What?"

"Who says things like untoward?"

"I do, and that's the English degree talking." He took another sip of coffee. "What if you paid me by posing?"

Her own swallow of coffee nearly choked her and she coughed hard, trying to catch her breath. "Excuse me?"

"It's nothing like what you think. No nudity, completely tasteful posing."

No amount of brainpower could stop her from blurting out "Why?"

"Why not?" He seemed mystified by her objection, did he not see her? The curvy figure she possessed always caused loathing. She worked her ass off to keep herself from ballooning. Her mother didn't have the same problem. No, the woman blamed Aggie's bone structure, and natural way of keeping on weight, on Greek ancestry courtesy of Aggie's father. Something she couldn't get rid of, but maintained with a healthy diet—after she'd gotten over her bulimia.

"Before I say yes or no, what are you asking for if not nudity?" Display caution, but don't burn bridges. Another thing a strong woman did, at least it made sense.

"I need a model for a portrait painting. It's just to get a body model. No nudity because I'm looking at faces, arms, and legs...certain poses." His words were carefully chosen for her, and they did the job. She felt reassured.

"How many sessions?"

"Let's settle on five and if you want to do more we can, or if you don't then it's good."

Five sessions in two months seemed perfectly doable. "What about utilities?"

"I'll cover those. You can even leech off my cable. I don't really watch television because I'm always painting, but I haven't bothered to get rid of it." So nonchalant, like it was no big deal to pay extra money for a service he never used. The life of an artist really was something else.

"Okay. When can I move in?"

"When do you need to move in?"

She couldn't help but smile, and he gave a grin in return. "How are you okay with all this?"

"It's not like you're upending anything. I still have my place, my things, and I like to help. Ask Trix. She stayed here for a few months before I started charging her rent. Plus, you're a friend and assisting me with my paintings. It's a fair trade."

"Would moving in this next weekend be too soon?" She knew he'd say yes, but the possibility existed her request might turn his happy face into a frown. People changed their mind all the time, and she hated to impose.

"This weekend is perfect."

With the verbal agreement solidified, only one thing remained. "Will you draw up our agreement on paper, and then we can sign?"

"Afraid I don't have anything put together at the moment, but a handshake is good enough for me."

A part of her wanted to argue, but instead, she'd settle for typing things up on her own and bringing it back over. Murph was proving to be very informal about nearly everything, which drove her a little nuts. After the mess her ex left her in, she couldn't afford to have things up in the air. Security came from signed agreements, from legally-binding documents…holy moly, she was turning into her mother.

"Then a handshake it is, for now." She stood from her chair and thrust an open palm toward him.

Murph put his coffee mug on the table, and his larger, paint-marred hand enveloped hers. The heat infused a sense of peace, rightness. Diving too deeply into those feelings would be a bad thing, at least, for the moment. She needed to stay on top of things, not fall for the first guy she met after Jordan. But she failed to stop the overwhelming gratitude welling up in her, the need to express it with more than a simple touch.

Letting go of his hand, she stepped up and wrapped her arms around his shoulders. He remained still for a minute, the scent of his laundry soap mingling around hers, fresh and citrusy. She briefly thought maybe she'd crossed some unspoken boundary, but then, he wrapped his arms around her back and held her.

"What's this for?"

She chuckled, fighting back the urge to cry. *Crying is only if you want something.* "For helping me, and being a friend when you barely know me."

"I know you."

"Like I said, barely." Aggie let go, and he did, too. Stepping away, she dared a glance at him and tried her best to wipe away the visual affects the comfort his embrace gifted her with. She needed to leave before she asked for more things without thinking. "I'll see you next Saturday."

"Yep, I'll be here."

Chapter Five

One week later, the security systems had been installed in both buildings, Murph cleaned out his supplies from Aggie's apartment and fresh paint coated the walls. She'd be moving all her stuff in a few hours. He'd volunteered to help but received a firm denial. This was one thing she decided to shell out money on, a pair of moving guys and a truck. Then she'd also promised to bring over a typed agreement for her two months stay for him to sign.

He laughed at the thought. She'd be shocked to know his lease agreements were loose facsimiles of what they should've been. Hell, he couldn't remember if Trix ever signed one. The guy living above her, a friend of his grandmother's, lived there for years and planned to remain until his heart gave out. No sense in putting in an agreement there. No, he rode the wave, and it treated him pretty good, most of the time.

Right now, more than good. The painting of Aggie in the cafe sat nearly finished. The second one, of her sitting across from him at her table, ended up a two-sided picture where he painted her afraid and hesitant. Those facial expressions were locked in his mind, and he loathed it. Loathed how she'd looked at him when he got lost about the cow shakers. They'd been in his bathroom in the medicine cabinet, and how she frowned, recoiling at the idea that he'd want to see her body.

She didn't realize how beautiful all those parts of her were, and her body...an artist's dream. The Renaissance painters would've given her millions for a chance to showcase the different facets she held.

A knock came at the front door and he hollered, "Come in."

Patrick poked his head in. "How's my soon-to-be-famous friend doing?"

"Alive and great. What are you doing here?"

Suit-clad and holding a coffee, Patrick strode into the apartment leaving the door wide open. The foyer door lay in the same position, the screen the only thing separating the outside world from them. "You haven't called since the break-in. I got worried, especially since you expressed concern about producing more paintings. Obviously, things have changed."

His friend's gaze drifted to the two easels near the front window. Murph had pushed the couch back, setting up a small table and his painting chair. The track lights were positioned to give optimal light at all times of day, which increased a halo effect he'd put around Aggie's hair in the first picture.

"Yes, some inspiration struck."

"Inspiration? More like a giant influx of creative energy. I haven't seen you produce paintings this fast before. What's the secret?"

"Nothing." Normally, he'd tell anyone who asked, but keeping Aggie's existence to himself seemed important.

He'd been painting her since the fateful day two years ago when they met, though, Patrick believed her to be a figment of his imagination. His friend always talked about her like a muse sent from above, which he'd been fine with cultivating.

Trix knew Aggie existed. Yet, he'd never shared where they met or anything. Those little pieces of information he kept close as if they were secrets too dangerous for someone else to possess.

"Don't even lie. You've got something up your sleeve. Did you get laid?" Patrick asked while throwing a punch into Murphy's arm.

"Sex is the last thing on my mind." A fib for sure. He had an erotic dream last night about him and Aggie making out in his kitchen. They broke the coffee pot in their haste to rip each other's clothes off, and he awoke to fucking his hand in desperation until he came. It had been pretty insane. "I'm 100 percent focused on the art."

Karma hated when he lied.

"Murph?" The sweet sound of Aggie's voice mingled with the squeak of the screen door as it opened and shut, echoing through the foyer.

"In here, goddess." Patrick parried, the man had a way with words. A true salesman and Murph hoped his talents would get the bodies to the upcoming show. Murph jogged over to the easels and laid a drop cloth over both paintings. The last thing she needed to see upon entering his apartment.

Aggie walked through the door, true to the word Patrick called her. Her hair swept up in some half ponytail thing, a pair of yoga pants and a large, baggy T-shirt that hung off one shoulder. She'd always be a painter's dream, everything about her. "Oh, sorry. You have a guest, and I'm early. Is that okay?"

He turned quickly, giving her a big grin to hopefully cover up the guilt eating at him for not fessing up from the get go on the big role she played as the subject of his art. That the reason he landed the show happened because of a picture of her, wearing a work suit and looking like a warrior woman. Strong, intelligent, and so courageous as she walked through the therapy group doors. Damn. "Yes, it's fine. Moving in early, late, doesn't matter. The doors are open, and the place is ready."

His friend stepped in then. "Good afternoon, I'm Patrick Vargas, owner of the Blue Gallery off Bardstown Road. My inept partner here is too dimwitted to introduce us. What's your name and how did you get mixed up with this guy?"

Aggie shook her head and chuckled. "I'm Agatha. Friends with your inept partner and he's helping me out by giving me an apartment to stay in for a couple months." Then her attention switched back to Murph. "Oh, I also have the lease agreement in the car. I'll bring it in for you to sign as soon as the guys get started." She reached out and shook Patrick's proffered hand, reminding Murph of their handshake-turned-hug a week prior.

The contact between him and Aggie had been shocking and evoked a huge surge of lust, he'd done his best to school his reaction and keep things platonic at the cafe. Did his friend feel the same strong emotions with her?

Their hands barely touched before the handshake ended, lasting no more than a second. *Guess not.*

Aggie smiled, reaching up to tug on her ponytail. "Nice meeting you. I'm going to get this moving party started."

Once she'd left the room, Patrick turned on him, the look in his eyes all surprise and horror. "You never said she was real."

"I never said otherwise."

"Does she know?"

He turned to adjust the drop cloth and ensure it sat correctly and wouldn't fall off from a breeze or anything. There would be time to work later. For now, he needed to start prepping two more canvases. "Huh?"

"Damn, Murph. Does she know that all your paintings feature her as the subject?"

No, she didn't. But he couldn't force the words to come out of his mouth, so he shook his head instead.

"You've got a problem waiting to happen. She needs to sign a waiver."

"What the hell?"

"I'm serious, man. All major artists have people sign a waiver giving them permission to use their likeness. It'd be safer."

The idea caused his anxiety to run rampant. What if she wanted to see the paintings? What if she thought him the ultimate creep because of it? What if he confessed everything? Too many possibilities. Too many problems. "It's going to be fine."

"You don't know that, and I'm not hosting a show for you so this whole endeavor can come crashing down. I plan to make money off those paintings and so should you. Making money won't happen if the art's subject doesn't want the world to see the pictures."

"It will be fine." This time he said it more for himself; reassurance was as important as the tangible things, like his canvas. "We can cross that bridge when we come to it."

Patrick shook his head this time. "Jesus, you like walking a tightrope. Okay, we'll play it your way...for now."

* * *

AGGIE DIRECTED from the top of the stairs, the front

porch, and the lawn, ensuring her furniture and boxes made it to the right rooms, placed appropriately. When she finally looked at her watch, nearly two hours had passed, and the moving guys just lifted the last box off the truck.

"Hello!" a female voice called out to her.

A glance to her left and she saw a woman with blue streaks in short pink hair jogging over to her.

"Hi," Aggie replied as the new arrival came to a stop in front of her.

"I'm Tricia, and I take it your Murph's new resident?" She stood with her hands on her hips and a half-hearted, close-lipped smile.

"Yes, I'm Agatha Kakos." Years of training in polite manners made her stick her hand out for a friendly shake. Thankfully, the woman took it, but it wasn't firm and solid. No, this woman shook like a limp fish.

"Nice to meet you. My son, Seth, is over there playing." Tricia pointed at a little boy with black hair cut in a bowl cut, sitting on the grass with a pile of Hot Wheels cars. Every so often, two of the cars would meet by hand-driven collision and sounds of make-believe explosions would burst from Seth's mouth.

"He looks adorable."

This earned her another fake smile. "He sure is. Murph loves him to pieces, too. Speaking of, I'm making a huge pot of spaghetti and meatballs for all of us tonight. We'd love it if you joined us."

Suddenly, Aggie got the sense she'd intruded on some sort of domestic situation. Murph had never mentioned his only female resident as a love interest, but she picked up on her blatant implication from the last couple of sentences. The last thing she wanted to do was get in the way or become some strange third wheel.

"Thank you for the invitation, but I'll be busy all night

Painting For Keeps

unpacking. And there's a sandwich shop a few blocks over I want to try out." Not a lie and a way to keep things in the safe-rather-than-sorry-department.

Tricia gave a genuine smile then, beaming wide. "Well, if you change your mind, pop in downstairs. I love feeding people." She walked off then, calling out to Seth before scolding him for getting dirty and wanting him to go inside to wash up.

Her attention went back to the movers, who stood at the back of the truck tallying her final bill, and she'd need to grab her purse from upstairs. They'd just handed her the receipt when Murph's voice reached her ears. "All done, then?"

"Yes, everything has been unloaded and now you can't get rid of me." She snapped her fingers. "And I forgot to bring the lease over."

He gave her wink. "I like how you're much more on top of things than I am. How about you grab the papers and I'll sign them over dinner?"

"First Tricia, and now, you. Both of you enjoy having company while you share a meal."

"Excuse me?" The hunched eyebrows and pursed lips gave him away more than his words.

"Spaghetti and meatballs? Tricia invited me to dinner. Said she was cooking up something delicious for the three of you."

He nodded slowly. Silent and looking anywhere but at her, as if trying to recall the memory. She'd seen Jordan with the same expression when she confronted him about the scantily clad woman in his apartment. "She probably meant to surprise me. Something she does quite often. Her way of paying me back for helping her six years ago and for not raising the rent."

"Really?" Why did a tone of jealousy creep into her

voice? "I'm sorry. Forgive me. It's none of my business at all, but I did tell Tricia I'm going to settle for a quiet dinner in my new place. There's a ton to unpack, and I have to get organized before Monday."

The haunting look in his eyes was back, reminiscent of an animal confused. "There's nothing to forgive, but if you don't want to spend the evening alone let me know. Being in a new place can be intimidating, I've heard."

Funny how he said that as if he'd never lived anywhere else. "You've only heard?"

"Well," he glanced back at the two-story building behind them. The setting sun behind them made the bricks look like they were glowing. "Yes. I was raised here, and I never moved out or went anywhere."

She didn't know whether she was sad to learn such a thing or more impressed by his commitment to the buildings. "Do you mind if I ask why?"

"No, it's because here is my safe place. This is the place I feel the most comfortable, and my illness can make life difficult sometimes. Hopefully, for the next two months, this can become your safe place, too."

She smiled at that. Again, Murph proved too kindhearted for his own good. "Does anyone ever tell you that you have a heart of gold?"

The beaming grin she got for her statement made her heart happy. "No, you're the first. But Grandma always appreciated my hugs."

"I know you're good at those, too." No reply was given, and for a moment, the air between them charged with a load of unspoken things. His eyes were hooded and she detected attraction, a blush stealing over her own cheeks at the naughty image in her mind. An image of a hug turning into something much more heated.

"Do you want one?"

Chapter Six

It had been almost a week since Murph had offered up a hug. Stupidly, offered a hug. She'd turned him down, of course, running straight for her apartment and sealing herself inside. He'd been too distracted by Trix's visit and dinner to bother apologizing. Add to it, Trix gave him a hefty dose of guilt since she told him they'd made plans for dinner a week prior.

His fucking illness kept doing this to him, but the alternative...the medication made things worse. When he took the pills, they killed his creativity. No thoughts of painting, no thoughts of anything. His doctor said he always gave up too soon, but with the show coming up, the last eight months without the pills seemed to be doing him more favors.

And even with Aggie being out of sight, she never strayed far from his mind. He imagined her as the squeak of the floorboards sounded whenever she moved around. These thoughts fueled him into a third painting. This one of her moving in, the courage in her face as she unloaded her belongings in a strange place. The effort took balls, most definitely. He painted her like a conqueror, stepping into the unknown without fear.

He kept hoping to run into her, a brief encounter on the stairs, or at least, a reason to knock on her door, but no luck.

So, he'd resorted to cooking. Something he rarely did. The casserole was almost done, and Aggie would get home anytime. Hard to live below someone, even for a week, and not become accustomed to their daily schedule. He'd covered the paintings, cleaned up his kitchen and living room, and left the front door open, so the smell of ham and potato casserole wafted through the air. The screen door creaked, and he tossed the clean T-shirt back into the basket of laundry he'd started folding.

The security system beeped as she opened the front door and he watched her latch the bolt and press in the key code. Responsible, a word he had started to familiarize with Aggie. She stayed focused on things, distractions minimal in her world, so unlike his own.

She was punctual and methodical, keeping to a routine without breaking it, which is how he predicted her walk through the door at six at night versus seven or five. He bet she drove the same way home and scheduled in time to get gas or go to the store, as natural as a normal person.

"Welcome back."

Aggie let out a yelp, jumped while turning, and put a hand to her heart, keys jingling. "Sorry, didn't mean to scare you."

"A girl needs a good jolt to her system every once in a while." Her words were supposed to lessen the guilt, but the jumpy tone kept it firmly in his gut.

He summoned up his courage to ask the next question. "Can I pay you back with dinner?"

"I don't want to put you through the trouble." Aggie

tucked her keys into her purse and started moving toward the stairs.

"It'd be no trouble. Dinner is already in the oven, and I made more than enough for two. I owe you a copy of the signed lease agreement, as well."

She'd taped it to his door on Monday morning before she left for work. Another sign he'd somehow upset her. So, he'd made sure to get it signed, copies made, and even placed her copy in an envelope, neatly folded like the FedEx Kinko's service clerk suggested.

"You made a copy."

"I did." He grinned at how he'd impressed her. The little things, his grandmother always believed, were the way to a woman's heart. "We also need to discuss when you're going to do the sittings."

"Sittings?"

"The modeling for my paintings. It's called a sitting versus modeling because typically the subjects sit for a few hours at a time."

She looked away from him, glancing up the stairs at her door. Then a quick sigh before she said, "Give me ten minutes to change and I'll be down. No promises on staying very long, though. I've got a couple client files to review this evening for early morning appointments."

He gripped the staircase railing, trying to hold in his excitement. The urge to jump, hoot and fist pump the air was close to overwhelming him. "I understand, and I won't force you to keep company with me longer than necessary."

Why did he sound so dejected? The curse of being him.

"I didn't mean it like that, Murph."

"I know, and what I said came out a bit more angst-y than I intended. You've got clients who need you. The bipolar brain strikes again. Maybe I am a masochist after all."

She reached out and touched his hand. The momentary contact nearly short-circuited his thought process, and he wondered if it'd be like this every time they experienced physical contact. "You're a sweetheart, and you're not punishing yourself, unless you count the long hours you keep painting. I'll see you in a few minutes."

The timer on the oven beeped, and he darted back into his apartment and to the stove. The only problem was the dinner had bubbled over. A complete mess littered the bottom of his stove and checking the temperature, the stove was set at four hundred and fifty degrees, instead of the normal three hundred and seventy-five.

He remembered putting it on the right temperature and everything. Now the dinner, his grandmother's famous recipe, sat ruined—completely, utterly, burnt to a crisp.

Embarrassment racked his frame and he slumped in front of the oven, not even bothering to turn it off. In ten minutes, Aggie would, once again, be treated to his capacity for creating a disaster.

* * *

THE DOORBELL RANG as Aggie made her way downstairs. She keyed in the code to unlock the security system on the door and when she pulled back the heavy wood, Tricia stood on the stoop holding a pizza box.

"Oh, hi, Agatha." She paused, leaning to the side as if looking for someone, which caused Aggie to look, too. No landlord and Tricia's smile turned into a frown. "Seth and I got an extra pizza from the delivery service, eyes bigger than our stomachs type of thing. I figured you and Murph could enjoy it."

Painting For Keeps

"That's super sweet of you." And awfully suspicious since Murph made dinner already, it was in the oven and almost ready. "I'll take it to him."

"Appreciate that. I have to run back over and monitor the munchkin. He can get into stuff pretty quickly." She pulled open the screen door and all but shoved the box of pizza into Aggie's arms. "Have a good night."

With those words, away she went, running back to her building. So, Aggie locked up again and headed toward Murph's apartment. His door stood cracked open, and she heard a banging in the kitchen. The air hung heavy with the smell of burnt food, and the thought sent her dashing in without knocking.

Murphy banged his head, once, twice, and then a third time against a side cabinet. He sat slumped on the floor next to the stove. The burning smell was coming from the oven. She immediately slid the pizza onto the kitchen table and moved to turn the oven off.

"Where are your pot holders?"

No answer, and a glance showed him completely sidetracked. He stared into space.

"Murphy!"

He blinked twice and then looked at her. "I'm sorry, what?"

"Pot holders. Where are they?"

"Drawer next to the stove." He pointed to her left.

She opened the suggested location and hoisted a pair of crocheted pot holders, opened the oven door and pulled out the burnt-topped casserole. A dinner, extra crispy. "Can you grab the door?"

Murph snapped to then, pushing himself to his feet and closing the oven door so she could step forward and set the pan on the stove top. "Is your dinner supposed to look like this?"

"No." He sounded so forlorn and lost. "I ruined it by setting the oven temperature wrong."

"It's okay. Tricia brought us pizza."

He glanced where she pointed to the box perched on the kitchen table, a now completely clean table. "Why'd she do that?"

"Said she ordered extra and they wouldn't finish it all. So, dinner is not ruined. We were saved by the neighbor." A very convenient save, but she'd keep the thought to herself. "Where are you hiding the plates?"

"I'll get them."

"No," she shook her head. "You sit down and take it easy for a minute." There were times everyone needed help and it seemed he did at the moment. The more he tried to take on, the more problematic things became from what she'd experienced so far. Looking around, it appeared he conquered the Herculean task of cleaning his kitchen and living room. Stuff looked near spotless, and she admired him for doing so much.

He did as she told him and sat at the kitchen table. "They are in the cabinet to the left of the sink."

The room went silent with the exception of the clinking sound as she pulled two black glass plates from the cabinet. Setting the plates on the table, she placed one piece of pizza on each—how she always served herself with the proper portion. Then she took a seat across from him. Murph stared at the pizza, fingers steepled and resting against his chin.

"What's wrong?" She could guess his answer, but the question still needed to be asked.

"I fucked up, again. Here I was, doing so well. Didn't get lost in my work today, pulled together a dinner with real food, and even took care of paperwork. Then I burn the dinner."

She shrugged her shoulders. "Things happen. You can't beat yourself up about them."

"I bet shit like this doesn't happen to you." He bit into the pizza, then rose from the chair and moved toward the refrigerator. "Beer?"

"No, I'll take some water, though."

He reached in and pulled out a bottle of Against the Grain G'Night Ryder and a bottle of water. "Here you go. Amazing, I can do something right."

"You're really worried about what I think, aren't you?"

Maybe he worried about how everyone perceived him, but lately, the focus had been directed toward her.

"And shit like the dinner doesn't happen to me, but other things do. We all have our burdens." As she waited for him to respond, she found herself not hungry.

No, her workday left her more tired than hungry, and she still felt uneasy in the new place. Thank goodness for Friday, she could spend time relaxing this weekend and getting comfortable in her space.

"Yes, I care about what you think. You're my friend and a fairly new one. You only make first impressions once."

She laughed. "You already made a first impression and a favorable one, evidenced by the fact I moved in here."

"I hadn't thought about it that way. Then I won't scare you off?" He chugged a few swallows of beer and finished off his first slice while she contemplated his words.

Sure, he'd acted a bit off, but since he'd announced his diagnosis, it was easier to come to terms with some of his more extreme actions. She found herself fine with them, as long as he remained nonviolent. Yet, most of his negative actions were geared toward punishing himself.

"You're not going to scare me off. If anything, I'm

more determined to be a good friend. Good friends offer help, so if you need any, let me know."

Smiling, he grabbed another piece of pizza from the box. "Thank you. I don't get offers like that from other people."

"I'm sorry your dinner got ruined."

"Don't apologize for something you can't control." He reached over and their fingers touched, a spark...heat bloomed between them and a flush crept up her face. Here she'd been trying so hard to keep her distance, to stay strong and keep space between them.

After meeting Tricia and the move—all a bit too much, too fast. She refused to do Murph an injustice by starting something, which would only end with both of them hurt, if her past track record continued.

She pulled back. "Force of habit, sorry. And I did it again. See? I have my own problems."

"You think apologizing all the time is a problem?"

Had to be. At least, she'd figured her constant apologies as one of the reasons Jordan left. "It's possible."

"I don't think so. What's really a problem?"

A question she didn't want to answer, but— "It's going to sound crazy, but I'm unlovable."

"I call bullshit." Murph's words came out clear, even with the bite of pizza in his mouth.

Aggie shook her head in defiance. "Nope, it's true. People leave me. They may have all the good intentions of staying, but without fail, they leave. It certainly gives me the impression there is something wrong with me."

"I'm afraid I'm going to need examples if you expect me to believe this."

"What do I get for dragging up these bad memories?"

"Best I can offer is a hug once it's over." No grin or cheesy smile accompanied his proposal, instead he looked at her with interested eyes, ones that communicated the idea he was ready to listen to whatever she wanted to say.

At the moment, she figured a hug would make him feel as good as it would her, so she decided to take a risk. A risk for friendship, and strong women also helped their friends…at least, being strong meant facing your past. All in the name of making Murph feel better, which was the reason she'd go with. "Fine, I'll take your offering."

Chapter Seven

For Aggie, these memories would be difficult on her, but she'd talk about them regardless. Where to start? "My dad left America and moved to Greece when I turned nine. He divorced my mother, and I remember they were having an argument about me. I'd pulled a bully's hair and got in trouble with the school, again. I was told to be nicer, more forgiving."

"What did the bully do?"

"She shoved me into a wall and called me fat. I retaliated. My father believed my mother's job involved taking me in hand, and when I refused to follow all the rules, he left." The memory of the day was burned into her brain, waking up to her father carrying a suitcase out the front door, her mother still asleep in bed.

There was no note, no hugs and kisses goodbye. He'd just left and broke her damn heart. "My mom stuck around, bouncing between replacement husbands to support us until my senior year of high school. Then she went on a cruise for spring break while I was working overtime at my job. She met some sugar daddy, married him on my graduation day, and took off."

Another burn to her fragile psyche. No graduation parties for Aggie. Instead, it had been a freedom celebration. At least, that's how dearest Mom, or as she called her now, Edith, referred to it. They were celebrating the freedom to live life as they chose. Really, Edith got to live the life she wanted. Aggie got stuck with whatever she could come up with on her own.

"We hardly talk now. She calls every so often, and we move through a perfunctory conversation with the same questions, same answers."

"Sounds awful."

"It's reality, and I've moved on, but then there's my best friend. June and I were joined at the hip…through high school, even into college. She meets a guy who introduces her to this church. When I couldn't work my schedule around to try this place out, more than a couple times, she ditched me. I mean, cut off all contact. No matter how close we were, she still gave up our friendship."

Murphy frowned. "These people sound like assholes, Aggie. Including your parents. I don't really think they left because you were unlovable. It sounds like these people took advantage of you and your quiet nature."

She tried to believe it, tried to so hard, but then, "I can sometimes convince myself they possessed selfish natures until I get to Jordan."

"The boyfriend who cheated on you?"

"Yes, if I'd been more, less needy, maybe he wouldn't have cheated on me." She'd looked at it from every angle. Several times during their relationship she'd been inattentive, less responsive to him. Her mother would have called that a serious lapse in judgment. "I stopped paying attention to him. We lost some of the closeness from earlier on, and I let the gap widen. I failed at communicating or trying to put the spark back in our relationship. I let things fall apart."

"Is this your own personal observation or something he told you?"

Moisture welled in her eyes and she heard Murph's chair squeak as the legs slid sharply against the linoleum floor. Before she could object, or even answer his question, he hauled her to her feet and wrapped her in a hug. The way their bodies aligned, in some perfect way, like two puzzle pieces joining together, hit her straight in the chest and a knot formed there.

This hug touched her emotional center more than the first one. She could easily blame it on all the memories she'd stirred, coupled with this display of affection. Jordan had heard her cry about her family before and always told her to forget them, live in the now with him. Murph did the opposite.

"They were assholes, and I know it hurts. But this hug is a good memory. One you can draw on when the bad ones surface, which they always do even when we don't want them. I'm not leaving you."

She squeezed him back, loving how his muscled parts fit against her soft ones. She was incredibly softer than he, but it worked. He held her tighter and smelled of pine and paint, a refreshing scent. When they finally pulled apart, more like their upper halves loosening the hold on one another, he kept his arms and hands entangled with hers. They'd shared something, a common respect for both of them being a bit damaged, a bit not-quite-right.

They locked eyes and for a moment, Aggie believed he'd kiss her. She wanted him to. Just once, to know what the experience of kissing someone who got her was like.

Instead, he said, "Let me paint you."

***

AGGIE SHARPLY INHALED, and then asked the hard to answer question. "Why?"

"You're so strong, fierce. I want to capture the emotion, the essence of you." Sometimes he surprised himself—the reason sounded decent. He also didn't want to let her go, but she pulled away from him and started pacing the kitchen.

"I'm really uncomfortable about showing my body to anyone."

He held up his hands. "No, you're misunderstanding me. This is clothes on, completely. I would never spring nude posing on someone as a fun, random suggestion."

That seemed to be the reassurance she needed. "Okay, where do we do this?"

He pointed to the living room. "In there. Feel free to take a seat on the couch or wherever...the chair even. You do what feels natural, and I'll move to paint you."

So she did. Grabbing her bottle of water, she propped herself into the large chair in the center of the room. He would've suggested she grab that one, just because the shape was more versatile to poses. She tucked her legs underneath her and propped her head in one hand.

He grabbed a blank canvas from his supply room, one already treated and ready for use. When he walked back in, she'd kicked off her shoes and let her hair free from its ponytail. She became the embodiment of his muse, and in a way, his savior. How could he ever tell her how she'd helped him, kept him from falling into dark places?

"Is this what you were thinking?"

Mouth dry, it took him a minute to respond. "Whatever is most comfortable for you. Ultimately, I'm at your mercy."

Murph concentrated on gathering his supplies. For now, it'd be his stool, easel, canvas, and sketching pencils. The pre-sketch essential to helping him line out the rest of the painting.

When he finally looked back at her, she appeared the opposite of fierce. No, Aggie transformed into sultry. Hair down around her shoulders, a smile teasing her lips. It was downright the exact opposite of what he'd expected, and he adjusted his pants and scooted away from his stool. "I'm going to fix the lighting."

He moved to the controls on the wall for the track lighting angles. One of the few alterations he'd made to the apartment, and desperately needed. For a painter, light proved the difference between a decent painting and a masterpiece.

As the lights positioned into place, he tried to think about something unattractive. Something he disliked, merely to calm himself, like rainy days or sunburns. This woman drove him to the breaking point. If he'd been a tube of paint, he'd have exploded from heat exposure.

"How often do you have models for your paintings?"

Finally, an easy question. "Never, you're my first one."

"That makes me a little nervous."

The last light finally in place, he moved back to his seat. "No expectations, Aggie. I want to paint you, any way and any how. I'm open to your conditions on this."

She laughed, a little self-conscience sounding laugh. The kind of laugh to sprout gooseflesh on his skin and send a tingle down his spine—a good one. "My conditions? Maybe I should set some."

"You can, if you want."

The way she phrased the sentence made it sound like she had something sexual planned, but he refused to let his mind wander in carnal directions. Easel set, pencil in hand, he gave his full gaze to Aggie. The lighting, now perfect, illuminated her hair and left part of her profile in shadow. "Would it hurt for you to turn your head a bit to the left?"

"No," she did as he asked. "Is this all right?"

"Perfect." As Murph started to sketch, his eyes took notice of things he'd not paid attention to before. The narrow slant of her eyes in comparison to her angular nose, the slender elongated neck, and even the elf-like structure of her ears were all new, exciting things to him.

Painting his muse in the flesh, even the sketching part, proved to be ten times better than what his own mind's eye could conjure. He found happiness here with her, joy. "So talk to me. You can speak while I sketch. Ask questions. You confessed plenty of things to me."

An audible sigh came from her. "Thank goodness. If I had to stay silent, this would have ended with me asleep."

Then she paused, taking a moment to think, and he used the opportunity to start a quick sketch of her lips. Those two pieces of flesh were perfect, a cupid's bow with a lush upper half, compared to its pouty bottom twin.

She broke his focus when she asked, "How long have you wanted to paint?"

"I've been sketching and drawing since elementary school. Then I went to high school and fell in love with the classics. College is really where I went head first into tempera."

"Tempera?"

"The ways of the masters. Tempera is painting with egg yolk, a simple definition to be sure. It also involves layering and building upon the painting with multiple colors. Da Vinci used to paint this way before he moved to oils. Oils, of course, became the technique of preference."

She moved, sitting up straight, which worked with the

lighting and gave a nice view of her neck. "Really? Why paint with egg then?"

"It calls to me, a challenge to fully absorb me. I also wanted to dispel the belief that oil paintings are more vibrant than tempera oils. A common argument, but so far I think between myself, and several others, we've got them beat." And he'd never been so fascinated by a painting process. It caught his interest and never let go.

"So you love it enough to make it a career?" He liked her interest in him, his life, and his hobbies.

"It's really a hobby. My main income is the apartments. They were left to me by Grandma, along with enough savings to keep me comfortable. I invested a little bit, and it turns out those guys at the investment firm place they advertise everywhere on the radio are pretty smart. I'm making money, not losing it. The show and everything is something that fell into my lap. It's kind of out of control."

Truly, it was. "I met Patrick on a fluke visit to his gallery, shared a painting with him, and he loved it so much he put it on display. Then he convinced me to do the show...seemed like a great idea at the time—until someone ruined all my paintings. Now, I'm starting from scratch."

"Why not postpone?"

Murph shook his head. "There are people interested in my work. Reputations are on the line, not only mine. For the first time in forever, I'm committed to something and it freaks me out, I guess." Pressing too hard on the canvas, trying to nail the curvature of her shoulder, the tip of the pencil broke. "Shit."

He reached into his pencil pouch for the sharpener and came up empty handed. "Damn."

"What's wrong?" she asked as she stood.

"Busted the pencil and my sharpener is missing." He set the pouch on the floor and the pencil on the easel. "My biggest issue lately is I keep moving things and I don't remember doing it. A bad side effect, I guess. Memory is playing games with me."

Aggie walked over. "Do we need to stop for the night?"

"I probably have another pencil in the spare room where I keep all my supplies." When Murph stood, the distance between their bodies disappeared. When had she gotten so close? Heat radiated from her like a slow-burning fire in need of a new log to stoke the embers. "Unless you want to quit?"

She had to look up to make eye contact, then her hand touched his chest. He inhaled sharply and froze. There were moments in time he'd recalled never wanting to end. This fell in that category, and yet, he knew he needed to say something, do something...intelligent.

"Aggie—"

"Hush, I want to do this. Just this once. I want to be impulsive like you are and give you a happy memory. Like the hug, except not a hug."

Then she leaned up on her tiptoes and pressed her lips to his.

* * *

IF AGGIE LOOKED herself up in the senior yearbook, she'd find the words "Most likely to follow the rules" next to her photo. Kissing Murph broke every damn rule; at least, the ones she'd wanted to stick to about taking care of herself, not getting involved with someone else. But she'd be a fool to regret it. Not when his lips were soft, different from the rest of his body. Not when she pressed a little harder, and he responded, fisting her hair.

A few more soft touches before he sharply inhaled. The opening, although brief, encouraged her to reach out with a tentative tongue. He reciprocated, and the meld began. Murph tasted like pizza, beer, and something smoky...delicious. She let herself get lost, as Murph called it. Getting lost refused to believe this moment was a bad thing, not when it involved his arms.

Lust rolled through her body, and she could easily picture this going further, involving the lights being lowered and both of them with fewer clothes. Reckless proved to be a very freeing emotion, one she should've embraced a long time ago.

Her hands began to roam between their bodies, down the hard plane of his chest and finally cupping his sizeable erection through his jeans. He moaned into her mouth and she pulled back, nipping at his lip.

Except, the hold he had on her hair and head remained, his other hand resting against her hip.

"Aggie, what...you didn't—"

"Shh." Leaning in, she reignited their make-out session.

She loved seeing him at a loss for words, out of breath and in shock. This, she held the key, the power, to make him this way. Imagine if he came completely undone by her hand or her mouth. The prospect was heady if she chose only one word to describe the concept playing havoc on her mind.

This time he broke the connection and pressed a soft kiss to the tip of her nose.

"Take me to bed. Let me touch you." The words slipped out, making her sound a bit desperate, but good sense had left the moment this whole thing happened.

The lust in his eyes drained away like a plug pulled loose from a full bathtub. He let go of her hair, of her, and took a few steps backwards until he came in contact with a wall. "We should slow this down. Take a minute."

Her eyes went wide and she clapped a hand over her mouth. The feelings, the wants, the him and her naked somewhere still existed. In her mind, a crystal-clear need, but he objected. After everything they shared in the last few hours, she couldn't stay. Not one more minute. Strong women got the hell out when a man rejected them, no excuses or pity looks needed.

She feared looking at him, feared she'd see the same gaze her father gave her when he left. The same look of pity Jordan cast at her from his doorway...the look that said, *I'm sorry but you're not enough*.

Murph stretched out an arm. "No...wait, Aggie. I'm not saying we have to stop."

No way would she listen. She started humming, turned and grabbed her shoes off the floor and launched into a sprint for the door. "I'll see you later, Murph. Thanks for dinner."

To hammer the point home, she slowed long enough to slam his front door behind her, before pounding up the staircase. Once secure in her apartment with the door locked, she curled up on her bed, a shivering, crying mess.

Chapter Eight

Aggie avoided Murph all weekend. He didn't try to talk to her or knock on her door. No, it seemed the kiss they'd shared need not be repeated. At least, that's what she told herself. Lips on lips, it had been one of the best kisses she'd ever had and turned from tentative touches to all-consuming within seconds. Tongues had joined the fray and then some roaming hands—okay, her roaming hands. The recollection of the muscles along his stomach, his rib cage, and package taunted her in dreams.

He'd been as absorbed in her, too, and then...no word came to mind in the last forty-eight hours to describe what the hell occurred. All because she'd asked him to take her to bed, he became completely unresponsive and wanted to stop. Where the hell her impulsive urge and words had come from, she still had no clue.

Way to throw yourself at him. Women let the men do the throwing. Yep, she'd hurled herself, and it had scared him. Scared, because during her endless analyzing and replay, she never recalled disgust or disinterest, but she'd taken it as rejection. Hell, she stayed away because of her freak out and her ridiculous behavior. In school and college, she'd played sexual relationships close to the belt. Never partying too hard, playing designated driver, and sticking to one boyfriend who happily got rid of her V-card. Then when he ditched her, as those around her often did, she'd steered clear of men.

Meeting Jordan had been a random chance and never would've happened if she chose to go home instead of out with a coworker to celebrate an impending marriage. She'd been happy, and a little tipsy. Jordan escorted her home, kept her safe. Two dates later, she'd decided to trust him with her body, and he'd made it worth her while until she became boring.

That thought stuck her with her the most, being boring. Murph inspired anything but boring. With him, she let loose, which freed her. A strong woman could make her own choices, and sleep with a man who she wouldn't be in a relationship with. Her mother wouldn't tell her not to do that. Creating excitement or a mood for seduction, not a common experience for her, but trying new things…she'd already done that by moving and everything.

As she parked behind their apartment building, she tried to think of other ways to get things between her and Murph back to less awkward and into more comfortable territory, maybe dinner. She could pull off dinner since she always bought more food than she needed. Maybe some pesto with the chicken breast, a little lemon pasta, and a bottle of wine.

By the time she reached the front door her mind was made up to invite Murph to dinner tomorrow night, then she heard the music—heavy metal, hard rock vibrating through the floorboards of the porch. Opening the front door, the sound blasted out, echoing through the foyer as she stepped in, slamming the door shut behind her.

The sound made no impact, and she couldn't believe Murph would deliberately do something like this. If it continued, someone was likely to call the cops. Punching the security code, she locked the front door and dropped her work bag against the wall.

She banged on his front door. No answer came, even after she beat on the wood with both fists. Ready to give up, she decided to try the door knob. So far, she'd learned Murph never liked to lock up or simply forgot. One of the reasons he suffered a break in, no doubt. At the same time, she couldn't blame him for people busting up his things. No one deserved property damage, especially to their own creative work. The knob turned with ease, and she gave a push. The force of the music hit hardest at the entry point.

Instead of trying to find her landlord, she decided to stop the wailing male voice upset with his breakup. She located the sound system in the living room and thankfully found the power button. With the music turned off she called out, "Murph, where are you?"

He wasn't in the living room, nor the kitchen. She tiptoed down the hallway, trying to shed the feeling of being a trespasser in his private space. The first room appeared to be a spare one. In here, she found a workout bench, a heavy boxing bag and stand, painting supplies, canvases, and a mini refrigerator—all around a general mess, which fit the artist part of him. The holes in the walls on the left side of the room disturbed her a bit, and she wondered if this room got his bad moods. Dread found a spot in her belly and started to grow.

The bathroom came up on her left, also open and empty. The space was small with only a toilet, single sink, and standing shower, but surprisingly neat. The exact opposite of the painting room. Finally, she reached the

Painting For Keeps

bedroom, and when she saw him collapsed on the floor, she ran over, anguish trying to grab every part of her.

She pressed a hand to his forehead, rapidly trying to think through the possibilities and keep herself calm. "You don't have a fever, are you awake?"

Leaning in close, she smelled booze. He reeked of it.

"What the hell did you drink?" She shook him by the shoulders, near panic. "How much did you drink?"

His eyelids fluttered and then cracked open.

"How many, Murphy?"

"Two."

She sighed, thankful to get a response from him at all. The next thing to consider—calling an ambulance. "Two of what?"

"Bottles."

"You're going to have to be more specific. Soda? Beer?"

"Bourbonbons." As horrible as it was, her landlord sounded precious and adorable slurring his words. "I drunks 'em." He struggled to put up two fingers.

"How do you feel?"

"Betterish. Aggie." He smiled and then gave a grunt.

The hand he'd used to show her two fingers now came and caressed her cheek in a lazy, loose stroke. While he fondled her cheek, she took his pulse and monitored his breathing. Being a perfectionist came with the perks of minoring in nursing and getting an RN. She'd long decided medical basics should have been required courses for dealing with people's eating habits.

His breathing checked out normal and his skin wasn't blue or pale. As far as she could tell, he didn't have alcohol poisoning, but her conscience wouldn't allow her to leave him on the floor.

"Am I really lovely?" She shouldn't have asked that, but

part of her wanted to know his thoughts without his normal checkpoints in place.

"You're uh-mazing."

Tucking her feet underneath her, she put both arms under his armpits. "Thank you for the kind words. I'm going to help you up now, but you've got to help me."

He nodded in agreement.

"On the count of three. One, two, three." She lifted, he pushed, and somehow, she got him to a standing position. Then they were both falling onto his bed. Thankfully, the mattress proved very forgiving.

Aggie stood and pulled Murph's shoes off, as well as considered removing more of his clothes. Instead, she opted to get him comfortable and retrieve a trashcan near the bedroom door to place by the bed. He snored lightly, falling into a deep sleep, and only then did she take note of his room.

A large, brown La-Z-Boy recliner in the corner with the matching walnut colored dresser, end tables, and bed. An old woven rug lay at the end of the bed, a basket for dirty clothes, and the brown flannel sheets. A closet in the corner held hanging clothes.

Different paintings adorned the walls, mainly landscapes, and then she gasped. To the right of the bed was a painting of her. At least, it looked a lot like her, the old her. She was smiling, wearing makeup and an outfit she never wore anymore because Jordan didn't think yellow was her color. How this image of her ended up on his wall, she didn't know. In a way, it made her feel special. She stood out in his mind, like the Cupid's Cafe letter said, she truly had an admirer.

Murph grunted and rolled over onto his back. Not willing to risk leaving him alone, because people died from choking on vomit or a sudden chill, the best bet involved staying here and checking on him through the night. Not really hungry, she snagged a bottle of water from the refrigerator.

After locking his apartment door and shutting off the lights, she curled up on the La-Z-Boy, grabbing a blanket from the end of Murph's bed. Wrapping the fleece around her, she set the alarm on her phone to wake her up in two hours. Enough time to let some of the alcohol get out of his system, and she tried to ignore the fact of how sitting in the chair proved more comfortable than any night during the last two weeks in her new apartment.

"Night, Aggie." His voice was a whisper and a comfort in the already dark room.

"Night, Murphy."

* * *

THE FIRST THING Murph noticed when he woke was his mouth, all dry and disgusting like stuffed with cotton balls. Then the lingering taste of bourbon, out-all-night-puke bourbon. The second thing was Aggie, sleeping peacefully on his La-Z-Boy. The foot propped up and her body stretched out, comfortable and at peace.

He wondered how she got there and couldn't remember much, though he did remember his argument with Patrick. The idiot kept bringing up Aggie and the paintings. No, he didn't have written permission to use her likeness, but as an artist, he'd always believed when inspiration struck, a painter needed to embrace it. Damn the consequences of the muse or model. While he still avoided asking for signed permission beyond their verbal agreements, the conversation loomed over him like spotlights in a display case.

Patrick resorted to threatening to tell Aggie himself

and getting the paper signed on his own. Asking for the rest of the week, Patrick agreed grudgingly and then hung up on him.

That's when it got bad. Oh, he went crashing hard and fast into a bottle of bourbon, which disappeared within two hours. Shot after shot, down the hatch, and he tried to paint his feelings, which produced the opposite effect. Instead, he cried, worried, and nearly destroyed every painting of Aggie he'd already started on.

The only thing to stop him was the wall in his spare bedroom. He'd taped his hands and pounded into the damn thing as if his life depended on it. If she said no to the painting, moved out, or worse...she'd think he qualified for the looney farm. Facing her, ruining what little they'd already shared, helped create the litany of holes. It'd been a long time since he'd acted in such a violent way. Maybe he was getting worse.

Murphy looked at her again, the slow rise and fall of her chest as she breathed. He wanted to touch her, impulsively anchor his fingers in her hair like the other night. The idea flooded his body with all sorts of arousal, his skin felt hot. Oh, he'd been such an idiot to stop things.

The second bottle of bourbon he'd downed to help him sleep. He'd been running manic for a while, and the episode yesterday was a mixed one. Mixed ones were bad and could get him back in the hospital if he wasn't careful.

Knowing the signs, he could ride this current mania for days, weeks. Another mixed swing filled with physical violence could easily happen again, making him not safe for Aggie. He possessed no good luck at all, the energy, the desire, the need for release still swirled in him. A hungry, angry beast.

When he left the bed for the bathroom, he heard her stir. A slow, soft moan trailed out behind him. He relieved himself, washed his hands and face, and brushed his teeth. *God, they need it.*

When he walked back into the room, Aggie had put the foot prop in its resting position and sat on the edge of the recliner. "How are you feeling?"

"Rested, but my head's really fuzzy. I may need some aspirin."

She shook her head. "Unbelievable. You really drank two bottles."

"Not my finest moment." *But one of his worst.* "Yesterday equaled a crappy day."

"I'll say. How about I get you the aspirin, and you lie down?" She stood and made her way toward him at the door.

"You don't have to do anything. Maybe it's better if you go." He needed to protect her from himself.

"A friend would take care of you. I'm a friend. Let me help."

"Okay," he said, stepping aside to let her pass. *You asshole.* As she walked out of the room, he followed her progress into the kitchen before he lay on the bed. He covered his face with his hands, struggling to find the right words to tell her about the paintings or ask her for permission, to warn her that he'd hurt her unintentionally. But it was like he'd been offered a chance, karma granting him the opportunity, proven by the fact she was here...in his place, his room. Selfishly, he wanted her to be the solution.

Oh, fuck. She'd been in here and seen his paintings, and most likely the one of her.

"Here you are, a bottle of water and two aspirin." Aggie's voice sounded chipper and happy, though how she could be excited about anything to do with him was a mystery. The whole thing made him want to groan. "What's wrong?"

And obviously, he groaned out loud. "Nothing."

He sat up and took the water and pills from her outstretched hands. After downing the pain relievers, he set the water on the nightstand, still searching for words, but perfect ones proved elusive. Instead, he settled for the obvious. "No, what's wrong is why you are here and taking care of me. You shouldn't have to pick me up off the floor in a drunken stupor or whatever you had to do. You certainly didn't have to stay, and it's safer if you keep away."

Aggie propped both hands on her hips and frowned. "Wow, you're a cranky hungover person. First off, I took care of you because, again, I'm a friend. Second, you told me you drank two bottles of bourbon. I found no evidence of the bottles, though it's not like I looked hard enough, but you consumed a cocktail for alcohol poisoning, so I stayed to make sure you stayed alive. Appreciate the thank you for keeping you breathing."

Now he was a bigger ass. "Thank you. I appreciate the help."

"Not so hard to say thanks?"

The look on her face, all stern and concentrated focus, made him chuckle. "No, and I need a good dose of humble pie."

"Good. Now we can talk about other things, like where this painting of me on the wall is from." She sat back in the recliner and he perched himself on the edge of his bed facing her.

"I painted it over a year ago."

"I like it."

He grinned. "You do?"

"Yes, it's a great likeness of me back then. I was starting to do better, opening up and things. Can't say I'm the same person now, but it's a nice painting."

"Imagine a whole exhibit of pictures like this one."

Aggie waved her hands in the air. "A whole room of paintings of me…horribly embarrassing. No one wants to see so much of Agatha Kakos. This body isn't meant for public display."

"That's not what I meant." *That's exactly what I meant.* "I mean paintings in the same texture and style, tempera."

"Oh, those will be wonderful. I like it. It's got this old, classic quality to it. Not like mixed media art. I enjoy classics."

Murph knew he'd fry in hell for what he was going to do next, but he needed her agreement. "A little confession, the displayed painting at Patrick's gallery is similar to the one of you on the wall, but it's a close-up portrait."

"Really?" Her eyebrows tucked downward and a worried crease formed on her forehead. He'd kiss it away if she let him. "Let me guess, this is the same painting that got people interested in your work?"

"Yes." *You, a painting of you.* The subject drew interest as much as the artistic style, but she'd never accept herself as inspirational. "I want to display it in the show, but need your permission, a signature on a model release, to do so."

"Sure, I'll do it if you do me a favor." The grin she turned on looked downright conspiratorial, like they were about to engage in something naughty.

Lord, he was on fire with the way she looked at him. He tugged on his shorts, trying to make room for his burgeoning erection.

"What?"

The grin went away and she looked at him straight-faced. "Tell me what the hell is going on with you."

He gulped…not voluntarily, it just happened. She put him on the spot and wanted the truth, which would most likely scare her away. Yet, she'd said she was a friend. So…"I'm in the middle of a manic episode."

"Okay, I'm a little familiar with those. What does it do to you?"

"It keeps me awake, makes me a little charged, angry, hyper, and I can barely sleep. Plus, I tend to talk a lot or think too much about things." He paused for a moment, trying to not be too excited to say the next bit, but he couldn't help it. "I'm also extremely aroused."

Wide-eyed, Aggie asked, "Right now?"

Murph could only give a single nod in response.

"Does it help if you relieve it?"

"I've never really done it to take care of the problem, so I'm not sure." His breath went shallow, and his dick throbbed in his shorts at merely the idea of releasing himself on Aggie. It had been a while since he'd done anything sexual.

"Then let me help you figure it out."

* * *

PART of her knew she should've been a little more demure or at least hard to get, stronger. Instead, here she sat throwing herself at Murphy, again. To be honest, she'd decided to do it yesterday, or at least play at seducing him. They could both take out a little of their frustrations with sex and the fact remained he made her happy, safe. Feelings she'd been missing since Jordan's betrayal.

Sure, sleeping with her landlord might be a bad idea, but they'd confirmed their friendship before he became her landlord. At this point, she'd passed sane thinking, and she'd justify any excusing thought entering her mind. She'd found herself wanting him nearly a week ago and since then, the urge only intensified, evidenced by the damp heat between her legs.

Her heart pounded in her chest. The air around her

thickened, making it difficult to focus on anything but his erection. The desire remained to recapture the taste, the sensations, and the thrill of their first kiss.

Murph stayed silent to her suggestion, so she chose action. Standing up from her spot on the recliner, she moved to the bed. She touched him first since he'd become a statue perched on the edge of the mattress. So still and breathing so slowly, she thought he might be afraid.

"Are you okay?"

"I could hurt you."

"How?" Such an idea seemed impossible to her since he'd stopped everything the other night. "You're the one always trying to protect and help me."

"I'm trying to keep myself in control, but I don't know if I can."

She smiled, somehow preventing the laugh wanting to escape. "You won't hurt me, and I'm fine if you get a little rough."

Normally, she'd never say such a thing, but Murph buoyed her need to take risks. He took them all the time—not locking his doors, painting, even putting his artwork in a show. She could be risky, too. Leaning in, she touched her lips to his, sticking her tongue out in a tentative approach. That's all it took.

In a millisecond, his arms were around her, pulling her tightly against him. She melted into the embrace, relishing how everything between them was as incendiary as the first time they'd kissed.

She dragged her hands across those muscles, letting them roam freely as he deepened the kisses. They were seductive, drugging kisses, and infused her with desire. He wanted her now as she existed. So, she'd let him have her.

His hands cupped her breasts, massaging them through her shirt before trailing a path underneath the rayon top to her bra. Those expert fingers of his unlocked the clasps in no time, and then rough, calloused painter's palms brushed her sensitive nipples. She moaned, and he responded by thrusting his tongue into her mouth. He mimicked what his dick would do to her later, like a piston in and out, before pulling away so he could whisper in her ear. "Take your top off."

Aggie was good at following directions. The top and bra came off, and she tossed them across the room. He shucked his as well, and she gasped at the tattoo she found there: a painter's brush with ink droplets spilling from it. Instinctively, she leaned forward to touch, and he hissed at her hand on his bare skin. "What does it mean?"

"That my body, my future, is an open canvas, free for the painting and taking." He refused to let her continue touching him. No, he lowered her onto the bed and covered her body with his, moving lower to suck a nipple into his mouth. She arched at the contact, the heat sending a wave of arousal coursing through her stronger than anything else she'd experienced. Her pussy ached, already wet. Sliding a hand between their bodies, she stroked herself, hating the barrier of fabric separating her from relief.

Murph stopped her from continuing, giving her a naughty grin as he stilled her hand, flicked open the top button of her slacks, and began to slide them off her. A slow, sensual torture as he traced the edges of her panties before removing those, too. In minutes, she lay naked and exposed to him.

Normally, she'd be trying to climb under the covers or shield herself from view, but all she cared about at the moment was his body. "Not fair, you're still wearing clothes."

"If I strip completely then I'll be too tempted to end

this fast." An index finger trailed between her labia and touched her clit, Murph's breath warm against her belly button.

She jumped. "This is torture."

"Then let me help." His tongue replaced his finger, flicking with precision before dipping lower and entering her.

The man possessed expert knowledge on how to use this part of his anatomy. The things he was doing to her she'd never experienced, from the way he nibbled on her outer lips, to the tongue twisting that found the exact spot to get her arms thrashing against the bed.

Part of her wanted to bask in the sensations forever, how her body was on fire with the ceiling fan's cool air giving a chill. How something tightly coiled inside her like a spring, pulled down, ready to burst at the slightest push over the edge. In minutes, she cried out for release, panting like some wild animal. She needed it, wanted to come so damn badly.

When he inserted a finger into her, a final plea froze on her lips. Her legs tightened and for a moment her vision blurred. Body bucking against the force of the orgasm, she screamed Murphy's name.

"Amazing, simply amazing." She fell limp against the bed, but Murph moved her so she received the cushioning and support from several pillows.

"We're not done yet." He smiled and reached into his nightstand, pulling out a condom.

"I don't think I can handle anymore." In reality, she'd never come more than once during sex, and anxious energy about letting Murph down coursed through her.

"What makes you think that?"

"Let's just say I've never been able to peak twice." She watched greedily as he removed his shorts, revealing his dick. Fully erect and jutting out with a little precum on the tip, the urge to suck him overcame her, to put him in a vulnerable situation similar to her own. "Can I taste you?"

"Maybe next time, I have to be inside you." A first time for everything since she'd never known a man to turn down a blowjob, at least not Jordan. Her ex preferred her mouth versus her body.

"Really?"

He rolled the condom on and positioned himself at her entrance. "I've imagined this for too long to stop now, even for something as sweet as your mouth around me. But only if you still want me."

His eyes, she saw the emotion there, the respect, radiating back at her. If she uttered a no, he'd honor her wishes. The idea sounded as foreign as refusing a blowjob, but then this man proved to be far more caring and giving than any she'd met.

"I want you." The word *always* almost slipped into her sentence, but she censored one of her crazy thoughts.

Brushing a strand of hair from her face, he thrust forward, and she pushed in the opposite direction to meet him, loving how he slid home without issue. They were joined in a perfect way. Soon, he started to move, slowly, and then picking up to a steady pace. A coiling pleasure rose within her, starting deep in her core.

"Faster." The word came out a demand rather than a question. If he increased the speed, they'd make it, possibly together, a goal for her since she'd never finished at the same time as her previous boyfriends. Somehow, the idea gave her thoughts of being inadequate. Yet, here she lay chasing a second orgasm. One she'd not thought possible.

He moved, altering his position within her by lifting one of her legs over his shoulder. The tension in her muscles mingled with the pleasure, shutting out any small pains the action caused. Their eyes met and she found herself locked on his gaze, both breathing in sync.

Too soon he cried out, and blood pounded in her ears as she went over the edge, too. The connection they'd shared moments before broken. It was perfect and safe...and like she'd planned, without commitment. So, why did her heart ache at the idea she'd given too much of herself away?

Chapter Nine

It had been three weeks since Aggie moved in. Two since they'd kissed and only a couple days ago since he'd first made her scream his name. Murph still rode the manic. Sure, the sex made it less intense, but he couldn't get enough of her. He even shaved so he wouldn't rough up her skin whenever he went down on her, which for the time being happened every day. She never stayed the night. Nope, it'd be sex, maybe a little talking, and then away she'd run.

Over the course of the days, in between amazing bouts of intercourse, he almost laughed at the word, she'd mentioned a food schedule, a healthy meal list, and even volunteered to pick up the groceries, if he promised to eat.

So, he ate what she bought, prepared the recipes she suggested and worked harder to remember to lock up, a problem she pointed out after their first time together.

Now, he stood in the kitchen making some healthy chicken and a brown rice dish with lima beans and cauliflower. Everything baked or simmered, like clockwork, and he tried not to get excited. Not about the release Aggie promised she'd sign today. Not about the painting he'd just finished of Aggie, passionate and desirable as she sat on his couch, beckoning to him.

A knock at the front door broke him from his emerging hard-on and wayward thoughts. He turned the sauce pan down to a low setting before leaving the kitchen, determined to make this dinner perfect.

He opened to see Trix standing in the foyer, Seth playing with a small bouncing ball behind her. "Howdy, neighbor. Where have you been hiding?"

Murph shrugged his shoulders. "Nowhere, I've been here and busy."

"Well, I made a pretty awesome pot roast for dinner and thought you could use a good, hearty meal. I know when you're painting it's hard to do any cooking."

Normally, guilt would flood his stomach for turning her down, but this time...no remorse at all since he'd started embodying healthy behaviors. "Sorry, Trix. I've got dinner already cooking and someone coming over."

For a moment she appeared surprised, even a bit angry. Her downturned eyebrows and pursed lips disappeared behind a smile just as fast. "All right, I'll bring you some leftovers tomorrow. Seth wanted to know if you'd join us for the farmer's market this weekend? They are having a parade or something."

Before he could answer, Aggie walked in the front door, smiling, black hair shimmering against a sliver of sunset peeking in behind her. Trix followed his eye path and beat him to a greeting. "Hi, Agatha. I'm trying to convince Murph to join us for dinner, but he has plans. Can I offer you a bite? Too much pot roast."

It was weird to hear Trix call Aggie by her full name. His original dinner companion smiled wider, if anything, the smile looked more painfully polite than genuine.

"Afraid I also have plans already for the evening, but thank you for offering."

He would've thought Aggie would move on upstairs, or come to greet him at least, but instead, his kind-hearted muse gave her attention to a little boy. "Hi, Seth. Are you looking forward to pot roast?"

For a six-year-old, Seth never talked much, but he looked up at Murph's Renaissance beauty and nodded in the affirmative.

"Awesome. You have a great night, okay?"

The blond-headed boy nodded again in agreement and then bounced his ball over to Aggie. She got the idea and started a small game of catch with him.

Trix's reaction to the exchange involved narrow eyes and the pursed look to her lips from earlier.

"Are you okay?" Murph asked while putting a hand to Trix's shoulder.

The venomous gaze she swung on him made him end his physical contact with her, and then as if a flicking a switch, it disappeared. "Yep, right as rain. So, this weekend?"

He'd lost any time to take a trip to the farmer's market, not if he meant to put the final touches on the three paintings sitting in his living room, almost finished, and really develop the next three. One of which he planned to start tonight.

"I'll let you know." The lie rolled off his tongue with ease, surprising even him.

"Okay, I'll swing by tomorrow." Trix's smiled disappeared as she looked away from him and started to move toward her son and Aggie, now talking about the ball in great depth. "Let's go, Seth. Dinner is going to get cold."

The pair walked out the door, and Aggie hurried from her spot on the stair leading to her rooms and plugged in the code to set the alarm system. Then she turned to him standing in his doorway staring into the building's entrance. She looked at him. "Is your oven beeping?"

Sure enough, it was, a steady, high-pitched tone pulsing out the end of his cooking time. *Shit.* He ran into the kitchen, turned the oven off, and checked the food. Thankfully, everything stayed perfect this time, not burned or overflowing.

"Disaster averted," he announced.

"Good. Because it smells delicious and I'm starving." Aggie's response came with her arms wrapping around his waist—so domestic and ideal.

"Did you want to go upstairs and change before we eat?"

She squeezed him gently. "Nope, I'm ready to enjoy my evening, not waste minutes changing clothes I plan to take off in a little while anyway."

A little tug with a twist and he'd turned his body in her arms to face her. Leaning down, he pressed a kiss to her forehead. "How do you know they are going to come off?"

"Call it a hunch."

They kissed again, soft and slow. God, he loved these moments when she acted as a fixture in his life, a piece of the puzzle. And truly, she fit into everything like the missing link in the chain. Things worked with her around.

"Good hunch. I'll serve up the plates."

"I'll help you."

They worked like this for the next few minutes together. A functioning team on the way to sustenance. Murph enjoyed having someone to share his cares of the day with, to review daily activities, and someone interested in what he did.

"Did you get three meals in?"

He scooped out a serving of rice next to the chicken

breast on both plates. "Yes. It's not too hard. With the alarms we set on my phone, I don't forget."

"I find it hilarious you barely knew half the phone functions." Aggie added the lima beans and cauliflower mixture to each plate.

"I'm not a techie; we talked about this. It's better to keep me as far away from technology as possible."

She nodded in agreement and moved to grab silverware. "Which I understand. Thankfully, your kitchen is already organized, so we don't have to worry about that, too."

He carried the plates. She grabbed the napkins and utensils, and they settled on his couch in the living room. "Want to watch a movie tonight?"

They'd fallen into a similar routine, too: dinner, a movie, sex potentially before, during, or after said movie. Most of the time she'd initiate it...he still held back, not wanting to push her or ask anything of her—ever.

"No, let's talk—about the painting, the schedule, or maybe your creepy tenant."

"What? Creepy tenant?" He focused on his chicken for a minute, cutting the breast into inch-size portions. "You mean Trix?"

"Yes, and what's up with the name?"

"It's a nickname because of her ever-changing hair color. Surprisingly, it's been blue and pink for a pretty long time, but won't be long before it mutates to something else."

"She doesn't like me."

He chuckled. "I can say I don't think she likes anyone."

"With the exception of you. She really likes you."

A feeling of unease rose in him. This wasn't the first time someone implied his tenant harbored a serious crush on him. Not the first time he'd wanted to shove it aside.

"You're right, and I'll admit I never talked to anyone about it before."

"Do you want to talk to me?"

Without hesitation, he responded, "Yes."

* * *

AGGIE SAT AS REQUESTED, back straight and looking to her left. A profile painting is what Murph called it, and truth be told, she enjoyed posing for him. Coming to his place after work every day and merely eating with him, being with him, kept her mind from thinking about Jordan or how she tended to screw things up in relationships in general. He made the interacting part easy. So, she enjoyed helping Murphy as a way to repay him for helping her not overthink things.

"You stopped talking."

Murph looked back at her from his canvas. "Sorry, I'm trying to nail down the curls of your hair. I never noticed the natural curl in the back."

"Probably because I've been keeping your focus on my front."

He smiled at her comment but went back to sketching.

"Will I ever get to see the final paintings?" She'd posed for at least three so far and he shown her nothing, not even a peek at the sketches.

"You'll see them at the show."

A show over a month and a half away, and she planned to be done imposing on Murph's hospitality by then. In fact, she'd avoided thinking so far into the future. No, she'd focused on the now, living in the moment. Her savings account was the only thing affected since moving in. If things kept going this way, she'd have the money for a place and more long before the two months were up. Maybe she could start paying rent here and stay. *Strong women pay their own way, unless a man is willing to do it for them.*

She wouldn't be her mother if she could help it, and if she didn't pay her way, she'd be like her in multiple ways. But how did she broach the topic without offending Murph or throwing his generosity in his face?

Better to discuss something else, for now. "How long have you known Trix?"

"Since grade school. We rode the same bus, but roamed in different circles. She hung out with a bad crowd."

"Like the cool kids smoking?"

"More like the kids on meth. She was drugged out from middle school on. Then I ran into her after she had Seth. She looked awful and strung out. So, I helped her, gave her a place to stay, a chance to get into rehab and get clean, and she did."

This man, who gave and gave, owned a heart of gold. Her own personal fears about being taken advantage of, or simple hesitation stopped her from being similarly helpful to others. Funny, his own troubles didn't stop him.

"Super nice of you, like more-than-normal-nice. And you weren't worried?"

"About what?"

"Your issues getting in the way."

He chuckled. "If anything, my issues, as you politely call them, make things easy for them. I'm the forgetful, idiot landlord with a very forgiving nature. I don't ask for rent sometimes, and don't make my tenants sign lease agreements. If they wanted to, they could take over the other building by possession being nine tenths of the law or some nonsense. But because I've been a help to them, they take care of me."

"How so?"

"Trix makes me food and my grandmother's friend on the bottom floor takes care of the yards, pest control, and any maintenance if I'm too busy to get to it. It works."

"You're lucky to have nice people around you, even if one of them is a little obsessive."

He focused back on the canvas, sketching away before saying, "Do you really think so?"

"The day I moved in, she made sure to tell me you had dinner plans with each other." It would've been easy to be oblivious if she were Murph. Simple to get wrapped up in a painting project and never see people closing in, stifling, or staking a claim—something that made her angry on his behalf. At least, that's what she'd call the emotion beating her chest.

"She's never acted this way before. At least, I've never had any women over, no one I showed an interested in, anyway."

But they'd kept their bedroom activities private. "How would she know?"

"The painting. She's seen it before, asked about you. I never told anyone you existed in the real world."

A thread of heartfelt emotion worked its way through her, sparking the hairs on the back of her neck. The first time she ever heard a man's voice in such a humble whisper. Almost as if he feared her reaction. "You make me sound like something special."

The pencil in his hand dropped and Murph moved to a standing position, causing his chair leg to scrape against the carpet. He walked over to her, slow, deliberate steps paired with his words. "You are special. You're inspiring."

Wrapping his hands around her arms, Murph pulled her to a standing position.

"You make the room brighter when you walk in. I breathe easier, and dealing with my shit is so much simpler.

Even in group, the conversations went better with you there."

She shook her head. "That can't be true for everyone, maybe for you, but most people don't think the same."

"Do you need everyone to think the way I do?"

His question made her blush. She wasn't selfish or vain and craved anything besides attention. "No. I just—your observations surprise me. I don't see myself the way you do."

"I said it before and I meant it."

She leaned in and pressed a kiss to his lips. A soft, gentle touch and she couldn't stop with one. Those lips of his always needed to meet hers for a second and third time, until tongues came out to mingle and get reacquainted. This time, though, she stopped things or else they'd never get anything accomplished beyond a romp on the couch or possibly the bed.

"Where's the image release?"

"Hmm," Murph leaned back in, his pursed lips touching hers once more.

She responded on instinct and then pulled away. "The paper you need me to sign for the approval to use any paintings with my likeness."

"It's on the coffee table. We can mess with it later."

Extracting herself from his arms, she clicked her tongue. "Unlike your tenants, who don't mind taking advantage when they can, I refuse to let you distract yourself from getting business taken care."

Searching on the coffee table, through a few small stacks of papers, she found it near the top of the last pile with a nice cup ring stain on it.

"This it?" She waved it in the air.

He nodded. "You don't need to. It's a formality."

"You've done so much for me, for everyone living here.

Let me do this for you, my way of keeping everything above board, taking care of you. Besides, this is for a painting on display."

"And the ones I'm working on."

That sentence came as she gave the last curlicue on the s of Kakos. "You'll be displaying those?" The thought made her anxious. She hadn't even seen them.

"Yes, all the paintings I'm working on will need to go on display to complete the show."

"People will only look at them, not buy them?" A little challenging for her, outside of her comfort zone by far, even more than letting Murph put her visage to canvas. People would see her, her body...they would judge her.

"The paintings will be on sale." This fact he imparted as he folded the release paper and tucked it into his back pocket.

"For sale? Why in the hell would you do that?"

"Artist's work at a showing is always for visibility and for sale. It's never been any different."

Dread filled her, bone chilling and with a gnawing sensation in her stomach. "Give me the paper back."

Chapter Ten

Aggie spent the rest of her week away from Murph, retreating with the signed image release form and her body into the solitude of her own apartment. He'd let her run and didn't chase her, which made her respect him and despise him in equal measure. She half wanted him to convince her to take a risk with him, to be reckless. Yet, she wanted to avoid people laughing at her, at him.

She'd been an idiot, naively believing a show was similar to viewing paintings at a museum. Beyond those musings, her anxiety increased thinking about people staring at her, breaking her apart as they would the Mona Lisa. What if no one liked the paintings? Even if one sat on display now, art patrons might not want to glimpse at least three or more additional paintings of her fat, stretch-marked self.

Better to spare anyone from such a fate, but she'd be lying if she didn't miss spending her evenings with Murph. Eating, talking, even sitting for him kept her strong and committed to her own goals. Not mentioning the sex...the sex happened to be the best she ever had.

Then, last night she woke from a horrible nightmare: everyone laughing, leaving, and walking away from her. Sleep proved elusive until her phone started buzzing around seven a.m.

The lit screen held her mother's smiling face, that different face.

"Hello." She left off the word *mother*, and didn't try to hide her exhaustion.

"Darling! It's so good to hear your voice. I got your text about moving, but I'm concerned. What happened to getting Jordan back, showing him what he's been missing?"

She'd forgotten about her mother's horrible suggestion right after the woman made it. "Nope, I don't care to go back to a cheating asshole."

"Language, dear. Bad manners and coarse words will never help you land a man to take care of you. Take Mario, for instance, rich as a king, and I won him with a come hither smile and my cultured background. You're capable, darling. Strong women, like us, are always capable of landing their man."

"Edith, I'm fine without a man. I'm doing well on my own."

"Really? You don't sound well. How is the landlord, the neighbors? Living near the Highlands is a great place to meet gentlemen. Have you been out much?"

Aggie rubbed her temples to stem off the beginnings of a headache. "Too many questions, let's go for one question at a time. My apartment is nice, the tenants I don't see too often, and my landlord has been helpful. As for the neighborhood—"

"Hold on there, Agatha Celeste. I heard a note of hesitation in your voice about the landlord. Is he attractive?"

Damn her mother for having some sort of superpower to ferret out any sexual or romantic overtones in even the least obvious answers. She could play dumb or just spill all the details, and that's what always got her in deeper with this woman. A woman who'd been one of her only friends and who'd fucked her up mentally at the same time, but Aggie never had the heart to tell her to go away. She did find the urge to not want to drag things out.

"He's cute, I'm fucking him, and that's it." *Holy shit.* She dropped the phone on the comforter and put her hands to her face, mouth in open horror. Her filter left the building and she needed to find it again.

She could barely make out her mother's words, frustrated and soft, followed by yelling. "Agatha! Agatha, where are you?"

Grabbing the phone, she held it to her ear. "I'm here."

"Good, I thought you'd hung up, which would have upset me greatly. You don't need to be ashamed at needing release or seeking it. After what Jordan did, I understand. You needed to be reminded that you're desirable, and you are, dear. But remember, a strong woman never gives more of herself than what is needed to secure her future."

"Edith." Aggie sighed.

"No, listen to me. This is where you went wrong with Jordan and I went wrong with your father. We gave up everything, all the love, all the emotion and they took it from us. I care about Mario, but I won't risk everything. You shouldn't either. Guard yourself, Agatha. Stay safe, my dear."

"Yes, Edith." What else could she say?

Another goodbye, a promise to call in a few weeks, and the call ended.

Hanging up the phone, she stared around her room feeling a little lost, confused. She needed to get out, away for a bit. She decided to venture to the Bardstown Road Farmer's Market, since it was Saturday. New stock, more vendors, and the best selection showed up at the market on the weekends. She was determined to select wholesome, delicious foods, and cook Murphy a healthy meal as a peace offering.

Maybe they could go back to their arrangement, no paintings or image releases, just sex. Sweaty, hot and oh-so-helpful for her battle against the real world. If anything, her conversation with her mother reaffirmed the positive nature of fostering a sexual relationship with a man. Even if a part of her deep down wanted to save him, to help, to be needed by someone.

Standing in the middle of the crowded market, she poured over a lineup of fresh mushrooms, bean sprouts, and peppers. It'd be ideal to make some sort of Asian dish. Maybe brown fried rice with thin sliced chicken or chicken lettuce wraps.

"Agatha?" The sound of her name, in that voice…

She'd never planned to hear it again. Turning, she got her second look at her ex and the woman who'd taken her place.

"I thought it was you. I could never forget the color of your hair or the way it curls—"

"Fancy seeing you here, Jordan." She balled her fists, willing the memory of her ex with his fingers in her hair to hell.

Jordan chuckled. "Well, not all my doing. Lucy wanted me to show her where the organic food is sold. At least the best in the city, and thanks to our excursions to all the farmer's markets when we were together, I'm capable." He hugged the blond, petite woman at his side and she hugged him back, all googly eyes trained on the man Aggie lost.

"Glad I imparted some knowledge to you." How those words made it past her lips, she didn't know, but the grated, painful sound of her voice was impossible to miss. "You know, I realize I left my wallet in the car. I need to grab it."

She turned and started walking away. Fast.

"Wait, Aggie. Let us take you out to lunch," Jordan called out after her.

Better not to respond to the offer. They'd already drawn the attention of a few folks thanks to her awkward reaction and abrupt departure. If she responded to him now, it wouldn't be cordial. Tucking tail and getting out of there, with a stop at a local gas station for something to dull the pain, was a much-preferred plan.

FIFTEEN MINUTES LATER, she'd fallen off the strong woman wagon with a bag of cheesy puffs and a half dozen donuts in her lap. She'd purchased everything from the gas station. Her car sat motionless in the parking lot and the driver's seat gave her a safe space to drown her pain. Each bite of glazed perfection dulled the anger raging through her. The first and second ones helped dry up the tears, the third, she stopped thinking about pounding her fists into Lucy's face.

After the fourth and fifth, she got a craving for salt and ripped open into the cheesy puffs. The crunch of the puff between her teeth, fake cheese goodness resting against her tongue, and she sighed in relief. Happy to be in a place once again without judgment, at least for a few moments, when she got lost in the idea that food loved her and provided more appreciation and comfort than a pair of human arms or a man ever could.

Jordan was not nearly as reliable as her junk food lovers over the course of their relationship. Halfway through the bag was when everything took a turn south. She remembered why Jordan left her, for being needy, dependent, incapable of keeping his attention, and most likely nothing like skinny Lucy.

Aggie lived in a state of overweight constantly. All the healthy food and exercising only got her down one pant size, and she struggled to stay in those. So fuck it. Two more handfuls of cheesy puffs entered her mouth and were swallowed down like sacrifices, meant to appease the black hole inside her; the gnawing thing eating away at her sanity and willpower.

After a few more handfuls, and another donut, she started her drive home. Each stoplight, she regretted more her decision to inhale the junk food. Her stomach stuffed and aching, all she could think about was how she'd consumed enough calories to cover an entire day's worth of meals and more.

By the time she'd parked her car, she'd already made up her mind, not like the situation hadn't been headed there, but still...she could've sucked it up and crawled into bed. Yet, as much as the awkward run-in with Jordan made her angry, her binge eating made her shameful—shame for wrecking her body in his name. She'd do best with purging.

Opening the front door, she took note how Murph failed to secure the alarm system again, a bad habit of his to be sure. Instead of privately taking her ready-to-puke-self upstairs, the very man she'd been thinking of sat on the bottom foyer step waiting for her outside his apartment.

"Aggie, I want to apologize."

She shook her head. "I can't right now. Can we talk about this tomorrow or later?"

"No, I don't want to let this linger between us. I feel like an ass."

"You lied to me, at least hid the truth about those paintings. Showing people is one thing, but selling them—

someone having me on display in their home...I can't." She ran up the staircase, clutching her purse like a talisman capable of warding off more harmful things. Not quite the conversation she'd originally planned on, and now her emotions were scrubbed raw.

Reckoning is what she was on course for. Once inside her apartment, she made sure to lock the door and headed straight for the bathroom. She'd get rid of her demons and problems in the next few minutes, take a hot shower, and then curl up in bed.

The purging hurt more than usual, burned more than it did in the past. It had been a long time since she'd given in to her personal crutch. Today made her hit the limit of her strength. Then, a knock came at the front door.

"Aggie? I can't let this go any longer. We need to talk."

Damn. The one time he got the courage to come after her, she sat at her worst. No way could she let him in.

"Go away, Murphy." The words came out choked as she gagged again.

"I can't go away and are you okay?" He'd heard her, which didn't make anything any better.

"I'm not feeling well. It could be contagious."

"It's a risk I'm willing to take. Let me in. I make excellent chicken noodle soup from a can and I'm good at tucking people in."

She hadn't experienced this side of him and damn her traitorous mind for wanting to. This was a time to be alone and recover alone. People generally wanted to be around women who owned enough strength to handle their own shit. "You don't want to see me like this."

"I call bullshit and if you don't let me in, I'll get my landlord's key."

She dragged herself to a standing position. Her throat was raw and ached. Water needed to top her list of priorities after she cracked open the door and proved to Murph he didn't need to help her.

Which when she did, he wedged a foot in between the entry wall and the door.

"I'll be fine on my own." Her voice sounded hoarse and ten times more awful than a moment ago.

"Sure thing, but I can start making up for my dickishness by taking care of you now."

"Fine." She walked away from the door and headed to the kitchen. Her will to fight him gone, replaced with the desperate need to soothe her aching throat.

He followed her, not asking questions, but waiting until she drank half a glass of tap water before he spoke again. "So, no stomach flu bug or food poisoning. What's really going on?"

She wondered how transparent she'd been. As far as she knew, her secret was still her own. "My problem, not your deal."

"Funny how when I said the same thing, you refused to let me get away with it." He pushed himself onto the counter, sitting beside her sink like it was a perfectly normal thing to do. "You don't get that benefit, either. Spill the story."

"It's a really long one."

"I've got all night."

* * *

MURPH COULD TELL she wanted him to disappear, if anything, to save her from confessing something he'd already guessed. She walked into the main living area and plopped on her couch, a brown leather cushy thing. He took a seat next to her and used the moment to familiarize himself with her, how she lived. Neat, tidy, and nothing out of place—the exact opposite of his semi-messy, chaotic living.

He'd never spent much time wondering at her habits. He'd always focused on her emotions, and it'd be best to keep things that way. Not waste time reminding himself how they were polar opposites outside of their sexual attraction and both dealing with a mountain of issues.

"All right. Lay it on me. I'm ready." He truly was. As soon as she'd walked in the building, he'd been ready for confrontation. Then she'd blown up at him and ran, which went against her personality in every way.

"I have bulimia."

He wrapped one of her hands in his. "Today you suffered a relapse, I take it?"

"Yeah, a big one." She pulled away from him, sobbing into both of her hands. After a few seconds, she came up for air. "I—I had a frustrating call with my mother and went out to clear my head. Then I saw him, with her, and they were in one of my places. Mine."

She needed comfort, whether she wanted it or not, so Murph scooted closer. Gradually guiding her body to lean against him, to give her strength in knowing he sat beside her. "Tell me everything."

"My mother is difficult on most days, always giving unwanted advice. She throws me off balance. I went to the farmer's market to get some stuff for a healthy dinner, food helps take my mind off bad things. The first booth I stopped at, my luck really, and he called out to me. Standing there with his new woman, the new me, the skinny, blond me. He brought her because I'd gone there with him. Making a place I considered safe for me awful and horrible."

Her whole body shuddered and another sob burst forward. "I got so angry, but I couldn't get the angry words to come out. Really, I didn't want to make a scene. For anyone to say look at the big girl he obviously left because she wouldn't lose weight or some stupid crap. So I took off."

Tightening his grip on her, trying to let his own body heat work as a balm, he asked, "What then?"

"Then I drove to a gas station and filled up on glazed donuts and cheesy puffs. Oh, I ate half a dozen donuts and nearly a whole bag of those cheese things. Shoving unhealthy stuff into my mouth, each swallow wiped away a little bit of the pain until I started driving again."

"Then you felt worse."

She looked up at him. "How did you know?"

"Every time I come out of mania or yo-yo from high to low, there's a moment I feel awful for anything I've put anyone through. It's like bingeing and then the purging. Up and down, the same thing really, and the moments before the down hits are all designed to take me to the worst possible place. A hole I may not be able to crawl out of. You just go through your cycles a little bit faster than me."

"I'd never thought of it like that."

"It's not an easy comparison." He tucked a bit of her hair behind her ear. "Actually, I came up with it a few minutes ago."

They both chuckled, and then she looked at him. Moisture still clung to her eyes, tears ready to spill with very little effort needed to do so. He had the strong urge to get rid of those tears, a protective instinct to keep her safe and secret from anyone or anything. "How can I make this better, Aggie?"

"Not much to make better. It's something I have to deal with. I fell off the wagon, and the count starts over again." When she stood a minute later, he felt bereft, as if something precious and warm had been lost to him. "I'll be right back."

Half of him didn't want to let her escape him again, wanted to follow and chase her down. He'd become tired of backing away, being quiet and reserved when the emotions within him wanted to jump up and over the moon. She'd done so much for him. Sure, he still rode a manic line, but the end wasn't in sight. No, in fact, he seemed to be coming down slowly, not diving into a depressive state.

Minutes ticked by and he glanced at his phone half a dozen times checking the time and making deals with himself, if she stayed away for more than five minutes, no, four minutes. Then he'd go down the hallway to find her, tell her the low point wasn't a time to be alone. Low points, like his a few weeks prior, required friends. He considered himself a friend.

Except, she walked into the room before the time deadline came. She crossed to him and came right back to his arms. "Thank you. I needed to brush my teeth. I had puke breath."

"I don't care about bad breath."

Aggie's single raised eyebrow nearly made him laugh. "Every guy cares about it. Personal hygiene is high on the list of desirable traits."

"Maybe for D-bags, never me. I'm here to comfort you with or without puke breath. Hell, you could have puke all over your clothes and I'd still touch you." He pressed a kiss to her forehead. "You're beautiful, Aggie. Inside and out. Too bad your idiot ex failed to see what I do."

Another kiss to each eyebrow. "You're gorgeous even after you've eaten a bunch of donuts or cried buckets. It makes no difference. I'm still going to want you no matter what." He rained kisses onto her nose, cheeks, chin, eyes, and finally, her lips.

Minty fresh taste assailed him, but it didn't cover up the inherent taste she possessed, something earthy and clean. He loved it. The emotion rattling around in his brain should've scared him, but instead, he decided to embrace it and pour every ounce of what he could only describe as love into worshiping her body.

To prove his point, he hoisted her into his arms, and she gasped in shock. "You'll hurt yourself, lifting me like that."

"You weigh nothing, goddess. Now, which room did you make your bedroom?"

"The one at the end of the hallway."

Twelve quick steps and they were there, a glorious environment of pristine white bedding, pillows, and a throw rug. The fancy four poster, queen-sized bed monstrosity even had a sheer white canopy. "You sleep like a princess."

"I like nice things."

His hands still bore the remnants of paint from his earlier session. His clothes were the same. The life of the painter—always messy, never neat. "Can your bed, actually can you, bear to see your bed marred by my dirty self?"

She playfully smacked his chest. "If you can stand all my imperfections, I can certainly handle yours. Besides, laundry soap and stain removers were invented for that exact purpo—oof." The noise, and her sentence cutting off, went straight to his groin as she landed in the center of her bed, exactly where he'd planned to place her.

He removed his clothes before joining her. "I'm going to give you exactly ten minutes to do whatever you want to me. I'm yours and at your mercy."

Aggie's eyes were as wide as flat brushes. "Why would you want to do that?"

"Because I take it no one has ever let you do it."

"No," she shook her head with the word.

"Then take your chance now."

She grinned, then a wicked, downright hedonistic grin. "Anything?"

"Anything at all, but when those ten minutes are up, the tables turn."

* * *

"YOU HAVE A DEAL," Aggie said as she sat up to look at him. Murphy's body was a thing of beauty, from the tattoo, to his muscles, to the thin line of blond hair trailing from his navel and surrounding his dick and scrotum. She reached for his dick first, loving the hiss he released when she touched him.

He visibly tensed, too, but never voiced any opposition.

"I missed this."

He cocked his head to one side as she stroked him, slowly. "What?" The question came out on an exhale, a sign she distracted him well.

"You, me, and a bed. It's been lonely the last few nights."

"I missed it, too." The softening in his eyes, the emotion lingering there, scared the crap out of her. She wanted no sentiments beyond the orgasmic kind, the kind to make them forget all the problems lying outside their building. The realities of their issues and the fact they both needed more help than the other could offer. He'd made her feel desirable in a moment when she felt the farthest from it. Focusing on the want would prove better than letting him in.

She bent and touched her tongue to the tip of him.

"Aggie, I didn't mean you had to do that when I said you were in control."

"But I want to." And she did. Tasting him completely and letting him fill her. He was circumcised and perfect. She'd always enjoyed giving head, but on her terms. Jordan tended to take over instead of letting her control things, but Murph, supplicant and at her mercy, she found herself getting involved more. Exploring. A wandering hand moved to his balls, cupping them and squeezing gently.

The groan she got from the action made her want more, and she repeated the motion, suctioning his dick into her mouth, hot and tight at the same time.

His entire body went rigid. "I'm going to come."

Exactly what she wanted, his cum in her mouth. Another ball tug and the swirl of her tongue around his length and away he went. Hot, salty semen pumped out, and she swallowed every drop. Lick and laving until his dick was as clean as when she'd first gone down.

He watched her, and she knew it...hell, she didn't care. "You are amazing."

"No, I'm a horny girl who likes sucking dick the way I want to." Or she was falling in love with a man who she shouldn't. *Don't give them everything.*

A chuckle, husky and low, came from him. "Really? Well, I don't think I've ever come so fast in my life." He glanced at his phone. "And right at ten minutes, too. Mind blown."

"No, dick blown." She winked at him and lay down beside him. "I feel better now."

"Oh no," Murph shook his head in disagreement. "The description won't do. I want you to feel as wonderful as me, and since those ten minutes are up, it's my turn."

He sat up and then moved to the end of the bed,

running his hands along her legs, massaging them. Not much time passed before he slipped the button on her jeans and peeled the denim from her, pairing the article with her socks, discarded to the floor. Her panties were next to fall prey and disappear. Then he started the slow torture, rubbing and kneading her bare feet, moving up to her calves, and finally her thighs.

She'd never been so aroused and relaxed in her life. Aroused because she lay naked from the waist down and at any moment he'd move up right where she wanted him. Her mind kept wandering to what he would do with his mouth, fingers, or both. Hell, he could've entered her, right now, and she'd be satisfied.

Relaxation of her muscles came from those magic hands. Her eyes went wide with anticipation when she felt and saw him start to trail upward, rubbing a single finger between her nether hair against her swollen lips. *Damn.*

"What?"

Maybe she'd said the word out loud and not in her mind. "I need you. I need something." Anything, she was so wound up, amazed she didn't jump off the bed like a jack-in-the-box or a spring released from confines.

"Something as in, an orgasm?" He smiled, playfully making fun of her.

"Next time I have your dick at my mercy, I won't let you come so fast."

"I'm worshiping you, not giving you quick release."

She groaned. "What if I want quick release?" The last word came out with a whimper. Pathetic, but at this point who cared? More worship meant feelings, and she already suffered from those, even if she wouldn't admit to them.

"You're at my mercy now, meaning no rushing." And he stayed true to his words. He teased her, flicked the top of her clit, pinched the same spot between his index and middle fingers before leaning down to kiss her. While their mouths entwined, he effectively demonstrated what his tongue was capable of. He let his hands get to work down below. Before long, he pumped into her with two fingers, his thumb grazing the sensitive area of her clit. She'd die if he didn't let her find release.

And she bit his tongue when he pulled out. "Damn it, Murphy! I need this."

He laughed. "I like you all wound up and feisty. It's refreshing." Then he pressed a kiss to her nose. "Do you really want me?"

The question was a loaded gun, the way he made eye contact with her, flooding her mind with emotion, chipping away at the wall of strength already weakened by earlier events. His stare so serious and filled with desire and something else. She'd been trying to avoid this, to not go deeper, but here he was bringing it up again.

"Of course." She looked away as the words came out.

He grabbed her chin, forcing her to look back at him. "Not a real answer. You didn't even look at me. Do you want me?"

When had everything gotten so serious? What happened to sex only? His question implied something more.

"I want your dick inside me, chasing oblivion."

"But me? What about the rest of me?" There was pleading in his eyes now, along with the other things, a crook to his eyebrows, and a worry mark in the center of his forehead. Need welled up within her, the need to smooth the worry away, to embrace him and remove all his doubts. He needed safety, comfort, and caring as much as she did. At that moment, she knew she wanted more from life, more from him, but getting it would be too scary to contemplate. Regardless, she could offer him a truthful, committed answer. "Yes, I want you."

This time he kissed her, and something changed. Their meeting turned into wild passion, abandon. She lost all sense of everything. And then, "Fuck. I don't have any condoms with me."

A risk, but she wanted him too much, wanted this. "I'm on the pill. Just get inside me."

"That's not...you don't know where I've been."

She touched his cheek. Funny, because she had an idea. "How many women in the last two years?"

"One and I've been tested since."

"I was with one guy and we never bare-backed."

"Does this mean…"

She sighed. Strange how they were about to share something they'd never shared with anyone else. "Yes, it'd be my first time."

"Mine, too."

Leaning up, she kissed him before whispering, "Then let's get going."

Everything went up in flames. She felt it in the way his body changed, relaxed and melted against her. Her shirt and bra disappeared somewhere in the mess of tangled limbs and tongue exchanges. Then he was nudging her legs apart, positioning himself at her entrance, and inside, she sang hallelujahs until he stopped moving. "Are you sure? I mean, I can stop if you don't want to risk it."

"I need you. I want you."

That's all it took, and he surged forward. Getting inside her to the hilt seemed easy enough, and she loved the feel. A brand-new experience without anything separating them. For a moment, time paused, and she let out a low moan of appreciation when he pulled out, only to gasp as he slammed back into her.

"Too rough?" He sounded genuinely concerned.

"More," she called out, closing her eyes as he started setting a good pace. Lost in the rhythm of their movements, she let the sounds of flesh on flesh and his fingers pinching her nipples to dominate. It didn't get better than this.

"Aggie, open your eyes. Look at me, at us."

She wanted to avoid it, but couldn't deny him. His gaze, strong and caring, locked with hers, and when she smiled, he smiled back. He moved faster, never breaking the connection with her. They rode the wave of their release, both of their bodies joined in pleasure as their orgasms crashed into them. The sensation of his fluids mingling with hers, a means of creation and yet release at the same time.

Murphy collapsed on the bed beside her, wrapping her in his arms and pulling her close. They lay there letting their breathing patterns return to normal. Aggie listened to his heartbeat as it slowed to rest. She started to feel drowsy, no surprise after the stress of her day and the physical workout. Murph pressed a kiss to the top of her head. A contented gesture, and one she'd happily agree with until he said, "Agatha, I love you."

Chapter Eleven

Murph glanced at Aggie lounging on the bed, sprawled across it. They'd been wrapped in each other for nearly twenty-four hours. He hadn't repeated his declaration of love, at least failed to see the need since she'd gone silent once he said it.

They'd slept, ate, and he moved on pretending like he'd never said anything. Better, though not so safe, since a part of him already wept for her missing declaration. The high he rode was starting to fade fast, and his buoyancy suffered. He'd set up a post off the left side of her queen monstrosity to take advantage of a bevy of afternoon light pouring in the south window. He put to canvas his love, sketching Aggie as she laid there tangled in her sheets, a princess on a bed throne; too unattainable for him or for anyone.

"What are you thinking?"

A question since he'd gone silent for more than ten minutes. Something he'd never get used to with a live model.

"This painting will be amazing because I've got a real subject instead of drawing from memory."

"It will be amazing because you are amazing."

He chuckled. "Always with the false flattery. Don't puff me up. I'm trying to stay grounded."

Rising on all fours, she crawled across the bed toward him.

When she reached the edge, she gave him a smile, a seductive, slowly appearing thing, bringing his dick to attention. "I can think of plenty of other ways to send you soaring."

"I like the sound of that, as soon as I finish the sketch."

Groaning, she threw herself onto her back, the mattress letting out a whoosh sound as she did. "How much longer?"

His hands were the ones controlling the time it took, and he moved faster now. Drawing the lines and shading the areas he wanted in shadow, the play of light and dark on the surroundings close to the bed. The bed itself would be pure white until it reached her skin, where he'd turn parts the same creamy, olive color. To prove where she touched everything turned, affected by her and her spirit—as he'd been. Yes, he was close to defining her hair, the lines of her shape, the folds of the blankets—

"Murph? You got lost again."

He blinked from the sketch and back to her. "Sorry, yes...almost done. Maybe ten more minutes. I'm just trying to get a few more details in here."

Then the fact hit him, they'd become sexually obsessed with each other. His body craved hers all the time. To get wrapped within her and since they dispersed with condoms —a risky idea, but one he'd too eagerly jumped at, his dick seemed to be at attention nonstop. Sex three times in less than a day was not enough, for her or him. Maybe they should slow down. "Did you want to get dressed and go for a walk?"

"Really?" One of her eyebrows perked up. "You want to take a walk over sex? Who are you and what have you done with Murphy?"

He laughed while his hand tightened around his pencil, nearly snapping it. *Damn*. "I'm still me, but I want to make sure we don't spend all weekend in your apartment. Also, this gives me an excuse to grab some food."

"You could've gotten that when you went downstairs for the art supplies."

Yes, he could've, but he'd been absorbed in his vision of the painting. As was his way, to get caught up in something to the point he forgot about everything else. A habit he didn't think he'd ever break. "You're right, and I got distracted."

"I bet I can help you get more distracted."

Then the doorbell rang downstairs. Not once, but twice. A Hail Mary from a visitor. Murph stood, shoving his chair back. "I'll get the door...and the food, sandwiches. Stay right there."

She laughed as he ran out of the room. He took the stairs two at a time and leaped from the top of the last three, his flip flops thwacking against the wood floor as he landed. Popping open the front lobby door, he was ready to face Tricia, totally prepared to confess he'd been busy, but instead, a dude with brown hair and a chiseled jaw, wearing a polo jeans combo stood there. He looked concerned at the sight of Murph.

"Is Agatha Kakos here?"

A rock dropped in his gut. "She's busy at the moment. May I let her know who's here?"

"Jordan, her boyfriend."

"Oh, you mean Jordan-her-ex-boyfriend-who-cheated-on-her?" Being nice was a better way to approach the situation, but this asshole had some balls to show up after hurting Aggie.

The ex bowed up at Murph's statement and took a step forward. "Who the hell are you? Whatever is between me and Agatha is our business."

"I'm her landlord and friend, and believe me, your business is mine because I get to deal with the mess you left her in."

"Murph?" Aggie's voice filtered down the stairs. "Who's there?"

He glared back at Jordan, letting the disdain and anger pour out of him. God, he wanted to plunge a fist in the asshole's face; a way to ease the pain of Aggie's silence about his declaration of love. Instead, he did the right thing and announced the asshole's presence.

"It's your ex." He kept the door cracked, refusing to let Jordan get a glance at their home, at her.

"Jordan's here?" She sounded surprised, and did he hear happiness in her voice?

"Yeah, I'm here, Agatha. Can we talk?" Jordan yelled.

This asshole. Murphy wanted to tell him to fuck off, but this wasn't his situation. He possessed no real claim here, only a friend with benefits.

"Murph, let him in and give me ten minutes."

"Okay, I'll let the jerk in." Yes, he threw in the last bit to be a dick. The thought she'd give this guy another shot hurt.

Stepping back, he ushered the A-hole inside. The main foyer didn't give much insight into their living quarters, nor were there any chairs to sit on. No, this place remained devoid of decoration on purpose. He didn't want it to appear welcoming, for unwelcome visitors like this douche.

"I take it she told you everything?"

"Yes, and you're not a very good person." Honesty, he had that in spades.

Jordan nodded, looking around at the empty green-painted walls. A skylight above provided the only illumination, which was a little, but not much. "Nice place you have."

"It gives excellent lighting for my paintings."

Murph's statement about his assessment of the ex's treatment of Aggie would obviously be ignored.

The douche raised an eyebrow. "You're an artist."

"Yep, and you interrupted my session."

"By all means, don't let us keep you."

"When you take away—"

"Okay, I'm here." Aggie's voice and her footsteps on the stairs cut him off from doing both himself and Aggie an injustice. But, boy, did Murphy want to knock the smug smile off that bastard's face.

Jordan openly admired her and Murph's hands clenched into fists, anger flooding his gut. He didn't spare Aggie a glance and kept the full force of his emotional frustration trained on her ex.

"Murph, can we have a minute?"

The question shook him, scared him, rocked the foundation beneath his emotional state. He'd thought they were coming to an understanding. She kept him sane, kept the monstrous beast within him reined in. Instead, she wanted time alone. Then came her hand, cool and alive, against his shoulder. Murph looked at her then, soaking in the pleading patience in her eyes.

"Sure, I'll get those sandwiches together. Just come grab me when you're done."

So, he left. Turned and headed for his apartment, opened the door, stepped inside, and then decided to leave it open a crack. To wait behind it, like a horrible eavesdropper and listen in because what if Jordan turned violent? What if her ex was a woman beater or tried to put his hands on Aggie? Those were the white lies he told himself to justify huddling behind a piece of wood and peeking through the slit caused by the separation of the door joints.

"So, you're sleeping with your landlord?" Jordan's opening line.

"If I am, I don't see how it's your business."

Jordan shook his head and leaned forward, bracing himself against the door frame. "Nope, it's not. But as a friend, I can express concern, can't I?"

Rich. Super rich coming from the guy who'd broke her damn heart, stole from her, and expressed no sympathy so far.

"Enough of the bullshit, Jordan. What are you doing here and how did you find me?" Aggie asked.

"I came to see you, after the other day…I felt horrible. I mean, I've been feeling horrible."

"About what?" Aggie's voice got low and tough. "Cheating on me? Stealing my money I put toward our place and moving another woman in with you? Going to a public location you know I frequent with your new girlfriend and praying you don't run into me?"

Jordan's face went red before he sputtered. "I didn't… the money, yes, that was wrong. I can give some of it back. I mean, your down payment at least."

"So, I'm worthy of a pay off? Is that what you do to assuage guilt every time you fuck up? You pay people money."

Murph slapped a hand over his mouth to stop his snicker from getting too vocal. His Aggie turned out to be a shark when it came to people fucking with her. If she believed herself weak, this proved otherwise. Jordan stood there practically trembling, but he recovered quickly.

"No, it's not about money. When I saw you yesterday, you looked so hurt. I couldn't...it hurt me. I needed to talk to you. I realized that maybe I was wrong. I talked to your mother and she gave me the address you'd moved to."

She scoffed. "Really? What about Lucy?"

"She's at home and doesn't know I'm here."

"Unbelievable." She threw her hands up before slapping both palms on the little side table. "First, you lie to me, and now you're lying to her. You called my mother, which is a big mistake. What a huge waste. I should've seen you coming two years ago."

"Now, you're not being fair, Agatha."

"More than fair. This is your clue to get the hell out of here. Mail me a check for my down payment, and never darken my doorway again."

Jordan stood straight then and plastered on a cocky smile, one that got Murph's fists at the ready. "Fine, but at least say we'll part as friends."

"No, Jordan. We're nothing. You guaranteed that when you took another woman into the bed we shared."

There were a few more words exchanged, but Murph didn't hear them. No, his mind focused on the end, the fact she'd severed all connection with her ex and now they could move into the future together. The door shut, and he moved into the kitchen with a little hustle.

Throwing open the refrigerator door, he pulled out the mayo, mustard, bread, meat, and cheese—time to enjoy a little lunch before their walk. He assembled everything and turned to find Aggie standing in the entrance, quiet and pensive.

"Hey there, everything go okay?"

"Murph, I need a little time."

"Sure. We can eat and then you can rest upstairs."

She shook her head. "No, I need to get some fresh air. I'm going to pass on lunch."

"But—"

"Just give me this." She left then, without a goodbye, a hug, or a kiss. He received nothing, except the sounds of more doors shutting behind him.

Standing there with a sandwich in hand, something snapped. Aggie was gone and wanted space. He'd done everything right. *You did everything wrong.* The voice inside fueled him, and the anger rose swift and furious. He threw the sandwich into the trash, marched down the hallway and into his spare bedroom.

Then he did a number on the speed bag hanging from the ceiling, pounding his fists in a steady rhythm. Minutes passed and finally the red haze started to fade. Satisfied, he went to get all his supplies from Aggie's apartment, determined to finish the painting he'd started, resolved to wipe away any remaining anger with blind focus. At least, until Aggie came back.

* * *

AGGIE TOOK OFF ON FOOT, leaving her car behind, and headed in the direction of the Highlands. Thirty minutes later she looked up and found herself outside Cupid's Café. Funny, the place she'd gone at the start of getting over Jordan, and after another confrontation here she stood again.

The cafe door opened before she could turn around and walk away.

"Ms. Kakos, what a pleasure to see you again. Won't you join us?" This from the too-finely-dressed Mr. Heart.

"Is there coffee?"

"There always is. You can even have your same booth. An Americano, correct?"

Aggie nodded and smiled before side-stepping past Mr. Heart and crossing the threshold. Immediately the nervous gut churning she'd been dealing with since Jordan showed up on her doorstep dissipated. A band played on the stage, a sign mentioned an open mic night, and everyone's focus was on the music.

Sliding into the booth, she took the side that had a view of the bar and the door, then sat back and enjoyed the atmosphere. Seeing Jordan again, watching how Murph stood up for her, and then living through how she stood up for herself…the whole experience left her a bit empty, washed out. She'd given everything she had into standing against Jordan.

Summoning all the rage, pain, and even her disgust toward herself and channeling it toward the offending party. When it was over, she'd known Murph had listened in. He'd gotten a front row seat to the whole conversation.

How she felt about him listening, she'd yet to decide, but for some reason she'd been embarrassed. A little ashamed by the idea he'd heard her anger, the way she'd turned into her mother. *Strong women never let a man get the last word.* She made sure Jordan left with his tail between his legs.

The waitress halted her musing by dropping off her coffee order, her Americano's thin trail of steam a welcome sight. She needed caffeine to help clear her head. She blew over the top of the cup before adding in cream and sugar. Then she took a quick sip, allowing the java to sit there for a moment, the heat on her tongue a welcome respite.

Within forty-eight hours she'd dealt with a fall from grace, being fully worshipped, a declaration of love, and telling her ex to get stuffed. Now came the challenge of figuring out what to do next. She wanted to help Murph, to continue to support him in his quest to get better and with the paintings. But did she love him?

"May I join you?"

***

MURPH PLANNED TO PAINT, to leave Aggie be, but he found all his earlier creativity gone, washed away. After what had happened the previous day, and her purging session, he'd feared the worst, that she'd go seeking solace in food when she could seek comfort from him. Why he'd decided to check Cupid's Café, he'd never be able to tell anyone, but it was the first place he went.

Sure enough, she sat at a booth inside. He saw her from the window, staring at the bar, her fingers tapping against the table until the waitress approached with a tall coffee cup. It'd be easy to just stay outside, watch her from afar and play sentry. Then the door opened to reveal Mr. Heart.

"Good evening, Mr. O'Shea. It's good to see you again. Can I offer you a delicious hot beverage on this fall afternoon?"

"Yes, I could do with a coffee."

"You're usual?"

Murph nodded and stepped inside, the calm washed over him and the fears he'd held of Aggie leaving or having confusion over Jordan disappeared. The courage to approach her welled up within him and then it wasn't hard to walk over to the booth. To catch her sipping from her cup, a small assortment of empty creamer and sugar packets on the table.

"May I join you?" The question came without agenda

beyond sharing a space with her. He wanted to be close, to listen.

She nodded, but still didn't speak.

He slid in to the booth seat and found a need to do something else. "I'm sorry for listening in on your conversation with Jordan this afternoon. You've told me so little about him personally, I worried for your safety and I also worried for myself."

"Yourself?" This, the first word she offered and it was tinged with confusion.

"Yes, myself. Being afraid for you is an excuse to justify my behavior. Selfishly, I believed I might lose you to him."

She scoffed. "Wow, you had such little faith in me."

The coffee he ordered showed up then, along with a bill, which he decided he'd happily pay. After being such an ass.

"Yes, I lacked faith."

"You sure the hell did. I may be weak at times, but I wouldn't let someone treat me like crap. Ever."

She'd certainly proved it, too.

"Yes, I heard and saw. I won't doubt your strength ever again."

They sat in silence for a few minutes, sipping their coffee, listening to the music from the latest band on the stage. The lack of discussion, the fact she'd not said one way or another if things were good, failed to stir any crazy emotions. Then he remembered neither of them had eaten in a while.

"Are you hungry?"

"I could eat," she replied with a smile. "And I forgive you."

Those words dispelled all issues, and from there, they enjoyed a fine afternoon into evening. Dinner gave way to the Mediterranean delights, more drinks, and that's when they started talking.

"What took you so long getting here?" Aggie spoke up first.

"Funny story. I tried to paint. Gave up, got waylaid by a nosy neighbor, wondering if you had a new boyfriend or something." Trix had approached him as soon as he walked out the front door and he'd waved her away.

"What did you say?"

"Nothing, I didn't even answer her or have the patience to deal with her. I just wanted to get to you. You make things better."

Chapter Twelve

"What took you so long getting here?" She'd tried not to let jealousy seep into her tone, but wasn't sure if she'd been successful. The idea of anyone else with him made her head spin, but she'd never admit to love. No, selfishness perhaps, but finer feelings needed to stay far away.

They'd shared a simple meal, with Murphy mainly wondering if she was okay, followed by listening to a guitar player and his accompanying pianist. Songs of love, life, and a fondness for open spaces filled the air around them. Nothing fancy, but calming all in the same.

"Anyone care for dessert?" This from the waitress who'd brought them fresh coffee only minutes before.

She shook her head on instinct, but Murph, who just came back from the bathroom, stood there with a hand on the opposite booth and replied, "Yes."

"I don't think I should."

"Aggie, you don't have to, but I'd like to try their baklava."

The comment made her a little self-conscience. She'd

never been a small girl, nor did she shy away from eating. Mealtimes, her favorite time of day, the one-time her parents never argued, the moment when they all talked about happy things. Food naturally became something she associated with good things, good times, and tended to eat too much during those.

"I didn't mean it as a bad thing, Aggie. Don't let your mind think negative things."

He'd caught her falling into the slump, knew her better than anyone else. "Easy to tell, huh?"

"Your smile turned upside down." He slid into his seat across from her. "How was the coffee?"

"The coffee is always good, and the company...even better." For some idiotic reason, she fell silent at that. Letting the fact sink in for him as much as her, she wanted to be with him.

Then his face embodied the same thing she felt, relief. Pure, sweet, and simple, and her shoulders relaxed, the knot in her throat dissipated, knowing she'd created good feelings for them both. Though, it'd be best to ignore the deeper meaning there, the underlying current of emotion threading through the room, the remnants of Murph's confession from yesterday.

The baklava came and Murph cut into one square with a knife and fork. He did everything carefully, with a grace lending to his volume of artistic talent. How had she not noticed how much time he took with everything, seeking the beauty in anything his hands touched? When he finally took a single bite between his lips, did she look away? A blush stole over her cheeks at the idea of him catching her watching.

"It's delicious, almost as sweet as you." He cut off another piece.

She blushed and tried to think of what to say next

without taking the conversation to an even dirtier place, and decided on a simple question. "How goes the painting?"

"It goes well. I'm almost finished with four paintings, only little touch ups and the final gloss to seal everything. They are ready to ship out."

"For the show?"

"Yep, I'll have Patrick come and get them tomorrow or the next day. Hard to believe I've only got a few weeks before the show. I actually think I might be done on time."

"Awesome." A sip of her coffee, another thought. "And the paintings you did of me, will I ever get to see them?"

He didn't answer her right away, causing a flutter of worry. Did he hate them? Change his mind about finishing them?

Then he finally spoke. "You'll get to see them. I promise."

"Oh, and I can't forget to give you the release back."

He opened his mouth for the final bite as she spoke so all that came out sounded like, "Hmm?"

"The image release. I took it because I got nervous about the pictures. A few of them won't hurt anything, as long as you let me see them." She had to know what the public would see. To judge his work with her own eyes and make sure she wouldn't be embarrassed. Images of Picasso's Cubanism, O'Keefe's modernism pieces, and Munch's expressionist pieces came to mind. Anything distorting and she'd rip the paper apart.

"All right, after we eat and head back to my place I'll let you take a look, as long as you promise to be kind." Funny, he sounded scared.

"Are you afraid I won't like them?"

"Every artist is afraid of rejection where his life's work is concerned."

The laugh that escaped her was more from shock than anything. "A few paintings of me are your life's work?"

"All of my paintings are my life's work. I've devoted my painting to mastering this technique, which isn't widely used. Can you blame me for thinking everyone will hate it?"

"No, I can't, but if you take as much care in your painting as you do eating dessert then I'd say you have nothing to worry about."

* * *

MURPH'S PALMS WERE SWEATING. They started when they left the café and was all about his agreement to show Aggie the paintings. A horrible idea, but one he couldn't see getting around as the bargain got him the paper, and her agreement to let him proceed with the painting. He'd worked for only thirty minutes or so after she left, and he'd gotten the last painting started.

The look of dismissal in her eyes when she'd left was the main driving point for the image. The emotion of anger suffused with a level-headed attitude slew him when he'd finally gotten over being a jealous, simple fool. She'd been wrestling with all the emotions and needed a friend. He could be that for her without letting personal feelings get involved.

Her bright smile, easy conversation, and her forgiveness healed him, drove back the monster and shoved it in its cage. He'd been moments away from bringing up the day before, the truth of his words of love. Then she mentioned the paintings. Skin clammy, sweaty, no sense denying how showing her this part of him produced more fear than when she'd left earlier.

They got to the house, walking arm in arm, the sun long gone.

"Did you leave the lights on?" This from Aggie as they came up the front steps. The house was ablaze with light on the first floor, the second remained dark.

"No, I don't think so."

"Did you lock up?" The question sounded a bit accusatory and he'd been less than attentive to the world around him today.

"Probably not." Dread suffused his frame and he froze in mid-motion. What if his paintings were destroyed again? He'd never be able to take it.

Aggie disconnected her arm from his and jogged up to the porch. Opening the front door, she stepped inside. He still couldn't move, afraid to face the magnitude of his mistake once more.

"Get up here, Murph." This she called out from the door, and he moved a few steps forward. "It's okay, everything is fine."

Everything is never fine. That snapped him awake. He had to check, to see. Reaching the front door, he brushed past Aggie into his apartment, the door wide open. Nothing looked out of place at first glance, but he could tell someone had been there. The chair pushed back, a blanket folded on the back of his couch—opened and balled up on the floor.

"Are the paintings okay?" Aggie asked behind him.

She hadn't noticed yet, failed to notice they'd been set up on easels in the living room. Three of his pieces were on display, covered in drop cloths, the track lighting off.

"Yes, come see for yourself." He stood, wiping his palms on his pants and sighing in relief. A small miracle whoever had been in here didn't destroy them, but the tissues on the floor and the crack in his glass end table top gave him a pretty good idea of the culprit.

Everything on display was painted during the time she'd lived there. Anything prior to her moving in was already packed and sealed for transport. No matter if she hated them, he loved each one. They covered the heart of his exhibit, and he smiled at them.

"Give me a minute. Did you know there's a broken plate on the floor in the kitchen?" Aggie hollered from the kitchen. He heard the clink of the ceramic being pushed around. She'd obviously decided to sweep up the mess.

"That's my mess, from earlier. You don't have to clean it up."

"Well, it's dangerous. You could get hurt. It will just take a second."

The thought made him smile as he started to removed the drop cloths from the paintings. She suffered from a need to do things. It made her a horrible posing model. Suddenly, an image of her kissing him, taking him right there on the floor of his apartment in front of the paintings burned a bright spot onto his brain. Stepping back, he switched on the track lighting, his art coming to life before his eyes. He wanted her to love them too much, to be as enamored and inspired by her visage as he was.

"You're out of trash bags? Who runs out of trash bags?" This time her voice, filled with confusion, sounded much closer, right behind him.

He turned just as she dropped the empty dustpan to the floor. The look on her face, her lips in the shape of an O, her wide eyes, and then her focus on the paintings on display made it impossible to gauge her reaction. She took slow steps toward them, with her eyes darting from the first to the second, and finally the third. He decided to eat up the silence with an explanation.

"My exhibit is called a study in emotion. I attempted to create paintings resembling emotions, in color and in expression. The first one is courage, denoted by the blue coloring. Some people believe blue represents sadness, but I think it symbolizes something regal. The second one is caring, with the pastels. I got this one from when you took care of me during my breakdown a few weeks ago. You were so kind, so concerned, and—"

"And they are beautiful. How could you think these weren't anything else?" She turned to face him and immediately wrapped him in her arms, tears in her eyes.

"Why are you crying?"

"Because these paintings do exactly what you want them to. I see the caring, the courage, and even the fear in this last one." The last one was her in the kitchen, his kitchen when he thought he scared her. Something he'd never do again, if he could help it.

"Thank you."

"No, these are beautiful."

"Like you."

She pulled back, half out of his embrace. "It's amazing you think so."

"Aggie, I know so. Let's sit for a second." Thankfully, she followed his lead and they both plopped onto the couch, never letting go of each other. "These paintings, the words I shared this morning. I love you, and I want to be with you. In a relationship or something a little more exclusive and official."

Her reaction first involved a frown, and then she got up from the couch and moved to the chair on the other side of the coffee table. "Uh, I get you care about me, and maybe we have become a bit closer than we ever were before, but a relationship is a little fast."

"Why is it fast? We're practically in one now. Domestic

bliss is much like this, right? You come home for dinner. I cook it, and we eat together before spending the evening in each other's arms or doing something else together. It's really just a formality of adding a label."

"True, but I'm not ready to label it."

He ran a hand through his hair and sighed. "Why not? Don't you want me? Because a little more than twenty-four hours ago you said you did."

The anxiety within him was on the rise, fast and furious, the manic, the frustration, hitting an all-time high. He possessed the ability to recognize it, and the knowledge didn't stop the mean words he let loose. "You're my savior, Aggie. You make the monsters, the demons I face go away. Without you I can't do this, and we make sense."

She got quiet, one hand over her mouth.

The words ran on replay in his head, he'd said them without thought, like an idiot. "Aggie, I'm—"

"I can't save you. I mean, I thought I could, but what happens when it's not enough?"

"No, it's enough."

"Really? There's a broken plate in the kitchen, holes in your spare room walls. It doesn't look like I'm saving anything, just stemming the tide. You left the door unlocked. Someone might have gotten in and destroyed the paintings. All this doesn't begin to cover my own issues. Even now, I want to stuff my face with something to wipe away the guilt, the idea I'm not enough. My mother was right."

He felt fuzzy, confused...like he'd fallen into some horrible alternate reality of his life. "What are you talking about? What does your mother have to do with it?"

"My mother told me to enjoy my time with you, but not give everything. I believed she was wrong. I could have you, be more than what I am. The truth is I need as much support as you, so I don't fall into my own personal hell. A serious manic attack, you being angry and mean, it wouldn't take much to send me over the edge. How can I save you when I can't even save myself? What happens when my love and care aren't enough? It wasn't enough for Jordan."

"This doesn't make any sense. We take care of each other. We apologize and lift each other. It's wrong of me to put everything on you. I can see how it would be a big task." He'd do anything to stop her from saying the thing he feared most, but it was too late.

"I think I better go."

"Until tomorrow?"

"No." She gave a single shake. "This time I'm going to move. I've got the money saved, and I'll be out within the next forty-eight hours. It may take another day or two to get all my things, but most of it is still in boxes anyway."

He stumbled toward her, fell to his knees in front of her. "Please, don't do this. Don't go. Give me a chance to show you. It can work. You want me, too, don't you?"

He lifted his arms toward her, like some savior on high, the only one to save him from the darkness coming. She owned the power to keep him from losing it. The paintings, a small part of him, but she'd become everything.

"It's not a matter of wanting." She moved his arms to the side, got up, and started to leave the room. "We're not healthy for each other, Murph."

Then she was gone, and he lost every strenuous hold he had.

Chapter Thirteen

"You're finished with the last one?" Patrick's voice droned in Murph's ear.

"Yes, just come and get it."

"And the image release form."

"It's signed." Not a lie, but he wouldn't tell Patrick the form wasn't in his possession. Hell, she could've torn it up and thrown it away. Yet, even at the risk of a lawsuit, he refused to stop the show. Any ounce of caring disappeared when Aggie walked out his door. It had been pulling teeth to finish the last three paintings. Forcing himself to bother with the effort. The depression hit, and it hit hard.

The worst days being the ones where he couldn't find things—paintbrushes went missing, his entire bottle of olifa varnish vanished into thin air. Thankfully, he had an extra bottle tucked away in a nook. Otherwise, he'd never seal the paintings. The idea he was in the middle of a delusion-episode occurred once or twice, but he refused to even contemplate going to the hospital until the paintings were finished.

Then there was Trix. She'd come by the next day with

dinner and continued to stop by ever since. She never commented on the paintings, and sometimes he'd never even hear her coming or going. In fact, he didn't care what the hell she was up to as long as she left him alone and locked in his personal hell.

When Aggie moved her stuff, as promised, he stayed in the apartment and stopped putting the security code in, in case she needed anything. With several finished paintings in the foyer, he secured the system now, not wanting to take the risk.

"I'll be by in the morning to pick it up."

"The door will be unlocked for you," he mumbled in response before hanging on up on his friend. Talking was overrated anyway. Now, he'd get lost in his thoughts and let the pain overtake him. Nothing mattered. Nothing at all. In fact, since he shellacked the final coat on the last picture, he planned to stay in bed until the show. He lay there in yesterday's clothes. Nearly twenty-four hours had passed and the bedroom was close to dark thanks to the disappearing sun.

He'd let himself wander the existence of his pain, mind still replaying how Aggie left. She'd never said goodbye. Not a single word from her since she made her exit his first night of hell, as he referred to it now. Two weeks turned into an endless mess of wake up, coffee, try to paint, maybe a sandwich, more paint, dinner of whatever, paint, and bed.

He stopped shaving and had grown some scraggy start to a beard. He changed his clothes when they started to smell, and maybe dragged himself into the shower if he happened to notice Trix giving him a weird look.

No matter the respective routine, the funk, the loss, and the need for a woman too scared to commit remained. Coupled with the wiggling, niggling thought in his mind she'd been right. He existed as a needy, dependent, crappy human who'd dragged her down with him, unless he got his issues fixed. If he wanted her, he needed to own his own problems, not expect someone else to save him.

His cell phone buzzed on the nightstand, and he chose to ignore it. Then he heard a noise upstairs, the floor creaking under feet, in Aggie's room. Reaching over, he grabbed the phone and answered the call.

"Hello."

"Mr. O'Shea, we wanted to confirm everything is all right in your home. We received an alert the security system has been activated."

The rustling and creaking of the floor above him happened again. "We're fine. Accidental set off."

"Thank you, sir. Have a good night."

He hung up and stood to tuck the phone into his pocket. For a moment, he let himself live in a dream moment. Aggie coming back to him, wanting to stay, and looking at the final painting with pure happiness radiating in her eyes. A look he'd seen only once before the ex knocked at their door. Before their perfect little existence got ruined.

Who am I kidding? Their arrangement screwed him from the moment he confessed his feelings. Damn horrible words he should've kept to himself. The creaking of the floorboards came again, and then something dropped heavy, right above him.

The painting. He'd left it up there due to better circulation of air for drying. The ceiling fans were on throughout, and if someone ruined it... *No!*

Launching himself out of bed he bolted for the door, not caring about the cold floor against his bare feet. Then a dash up the stairs, he really needed to turn on the damn heater. October had turned chilly in the last week or so.

There were no lights on upstairs, but the door to Aggie's apartment stood wide open. He slowed as he neared the top step. Empty hands meant nothing to bash an intruder with. *Fuck.*

No matter, he'd use his fists. He wanted to use them if the painting sat ruined and with his luck it would be. Another part of his life destroyed by his lack of focus and reluctance to get help of the medicinal variety.

A new noise this time, what sounded like paint squeezing out of a tube, followed by a whispered, "Crap."

Murph moved into the apartment and made his way back to Aggie's bedroom. She'd taken everything already, no furniture impeded his ability to get across the living room and down the small hall. He knew the creaks in the wood better than anyone and stepped in all the right places.

As he reached the doorway, he snaked his hand around the corner and flipped the switch.

Trix, her newly dyed green hair and wearing black attire, froze. The painting palette in her hand fell to the floor, splattering five different colors across the wood, her booted feet, and his bare ones.

"What the hell are you doing up here?"

She had a cat caught with the canary look. "I'm decorating the room."

"Really, then why were you inches away from my painting with a brush in your hand? You better drop it, too, if you know what's good for you."

She gripped the brush tighter and then started moved toward him. "I thought you'd appreciate a little added color to this room. The same room she stayed in, the room you slept in with her."

The words sounded vengeful, mean, and she offered him the brush.

"You should do it, not me. Paint over her, get her out."

"How did you know we slept together?"

She smiled at him, a sad, malicious look. "Rick's apartment. I clean for him once a week. Sundays. I saw you two with a pair of binoculars. You were both naked. She took advantage of you, sleeping with you for a place to stay. We have to get rid of her."

"No, Trix. She's gone."

Pointing at the painting, she crouched and scooped up a glob of paint onto the brush. "Not true. The canvas, her image, means she's still here. We have to get rid of her."

She launched herself toward the canvas and then Murphy shot into action, grabbing her by the shoulders, before sliding his hands down to lock her in place. He turned them both away from the painting and pushed her into the hallway.

She fell to the floor sobbing, "Oh, Murphy, I'm so sorry. It's just…she ruined you. She made you a mess, and I wanted to get rid of her for us. This painting, her nearly naked, it's an abomination. I can't even imagine how painful it was to finish, but I'm here to make it right. To save you. It's what I do."

He sighed, trying to calm himself. "How will destroying this work of art save me?"

"It will purge her from our lives. Once and for all. The other paintings are all gone. This is the only one left, and I can get rid of it. Then you can move on, and we can be together."

"I thought we talked about that." He crouched next to her, in case she decided to move toward the room again.

"Yes, but you never saw how much you needed me. Now, you do. You lose things when I'm not around, and you don't eat if I'm not cooking for you. I can take care of things."

He used a thumb to wipe away one of her tears. "How about we talk some more downstairs?"

"All right, but once I explain, you'll let me back up here to take care of this awful thing, won't you?"

He refused to lie to her about anything. "Let's talk first."

They made their way downstairs, and she seemed to be calm as long as he kept a hand on her. The moment he pulled away, she started to breathe heavy and panicky. Once in his living room, he sat her down on the couch and took up residence on the coffee table, cradling her hands between his.

"First, Trix, where's Seth?"

"He's asleep."

Good. The boy didn't need to be submitted to this kind of behavior. Plus, the next steps would be difficult. "Now, what were you talking about upstairs, the part about needing you?"

"Well, you do need me. You're getting worse and you need someone to take care of you all the time. Your condition can be very volatile. Losing your varnish and misplacing those brushes. It's like before Aggie moved in, and shortly after— burning your casserole dinner, and the shakers disappearing." She gave a sad smile. "I can fix all those things. I know where everything is and how to take care of you."

The problem with her little confession was he'd never told her about the things missing. "How did you know I misplaced those things?"

He feared the answer, worried Aggie accurately predicted Trix's obsession, but much worse.

"I took them, of course. You needed to see how bad it can get and the best way to prove something is by taking action. Like when you got busy moving things around in your spare bedroom, you forgot the alarm system and I walked right in. The oven, such an easy way to cause a mess, it could have been worse."

He tried to school his expressions, to not look horrified at her confession. "Anything else I should know?"

"I tried to keep Agatha out of our life before when I thought she wasn't real. The break in, all me, and I got those paintings out of our lives. Only you brought the real woman in. I realized you were under her spell, but knew she'd be bad from the moment I met her. We get rid of the final painting and everything will be back to normal."

"I don't think it will change anything, Trix." He pulled her forward and hugged her. She may not believe anyone, but she needed help. "I'm going to make a phone call real quick, and then I'll be back. Can you promise me you'll stay here?"

She nodded in agreement and then as he started to move away she spoke, "I hadn't seen you look at me like that since before Seth was born. It's taken over six years to get that look back in your eyes."

"Stay there."

* * *

THE NEW PLACE still didn't feel like home or smell like it, either. Aggie missed the old apartment with its gas stove and creaky, cold-in-the-morning floors. Yet, she refused to give in. No, her strength and determination were never stronger. She'd overcome her lustful thoughts and started working on getting better, which included signing up for one-on-one therapy.

No more keeping the problems to herself. She was getting her emotions under control. A few sessions in, she figured out she hadn't been in the healthiest of places. Not when it came to her past, her present, and everything she'd dealt with.

Yet, no matter how many days passed, how many healthy meals she made, or the number of clients she took on, she still dreamt of Murph. Moments of happiness and sexual bliss replaced with his pleading words and then the look, the destroyed, fall apart facial expression. He'd cried and begged her to stay, to give them a chance. But she needed to save herself, and he'd have to do the same. *Strong women rely on themselves.* Her new mantra, one to battle her mother's poison.

Her cell phone buzzed next to her. *Speak of the devil.* "Hi, Edith."

"Agatha, I haven't heard from you in weeks. Just some random text to not give out your personal information. What is going on?"

A tiny twinge of guilt lodged itself in her chest for not being very communicative, but Aggie still held some anger at her mother for getting involved in her relationships and giving Jordan her address at Murph's. Where did she begin?

"I've needed some time to take care of things. After you gave Jordan my address, life got complicated."

"You didn't go back to him, did you?"

"No, Edith. I informed him I wanted my money back and kicked him to the curb, not before I lost control and my had to start my recount over again."

"Agatha." The tone her mother used, she could picture the woman in her head, blond hair perfectly curled. Those same curls bouncing as she gave Aggie a shake of her head in disappointment. "You have to possess better control. Strong women don't let men dictate their actions. We dictate theirs. I still have no clue how you can even eat so much—"

"Because of you."

"Excuse me?"

Her therapist suggested confronting the fears she faced due to her mother, the abuse she'd suffered. Mentally, the woman who birthed her helped manifest the disorder she wrestled with.

"You heard me. I'm partially this way because of you and your twisted words. The poison of having to be a strong woman, of looking pretty, but being so hungry I needed to stuff my face. To never being skinny enough to get a man and getting lost in how good a slice of angel food cake tasted because food never made me feel like I wasn't good enough for it."

"A woman owns her own issues, Agatha."

"Really? Have you ever owned yours? You'd never admit to being wrong, to treating me poorly, and mentally jacking me up to the point where I'd do anything to be needed, wanted, loved, and only one person in my life has ever given me that!" She clicked the off button before a response could be formulated.

Breathing heavily, she grabbed a spoon and stirred the Greek lemon and chicken soup in the pot on the stove before turning it off and covering with a lid. Mission accomplished, but not completely resolved. There'd be plenty more rough conversations ahead of her, especially when it came to expressing her feelings without exploding.

She'd just turned her phone off completely when a knock came at her door. For a moment, her heart pounded in her chest, and a little anxiety rose, buoyed by the idea Murph finally decided to show up to talk. No phone call or warning, just to tempt her, and she didn't want to answer.

Another knock, this one louder, followed with a male voice, not Murph's, "Ms. Kakos? I saw your car out front. I really need to speak with you, if you have a moment."

Getting out of her chair, she tried to place the voice. It hovered on the periphery of her memory, and then she peeked through the peephole. Patrick, the gallery owner, stood on her stoop, bundled against the chilly night and looking like he was on some mission of mercy.

She left the chain and opened the top lock, cracking the door open enough to communicate without muffling. "If this is a ploy to get me to come see Murphy, you're talking to the wrong woman."

He held up both hands in surrender. "Not in the least. I come in peace for a piece of paper."

"What paper?" She opened the door a little farther now, the chain prohibiting any additional movement.

"The image release you signed and then held hostage. We need it before the show this Wednesday."

She remembered the paper, folded up and tucked into her purse. The goal had been to mail it, and she'd put the task off, due to a subconscious hope Murph would show up himself for it. "Hold on."

Shutting the door, she removed the chain and then welcomed him inside.

"It will take me a minute to dig in my purse for it. No sense in you freezing out there while you wait."

"Thank you," Patrick stepped in, shut the door, but stayed in the entryway.

"I can't believe it's already time for the show."

"Is that really what you want to ask me?"

No. "It's polite conversation." She opened her purse, positioned on a table across from the door and started moving things around. "I'm trained in polite conversation."

"Yes, well, I can tell you, he'll ask me much more invasive questions when I tell him I got the paper from you."

The damn man should get an award for piquing a person's curiosity. "What kind of questions?"

"How she had her hair and what was she wearing will probably be starters." Of course, he'd want to know, so he could picture it. Probably, he'd paint a picture to put a visual to the mind's conjure.

She found several papers and pulled them all out. Going through each would be a pain, but the faster she got this done the faster the torture would end. Unfortunately, she couldn't put off her questions any longer. "Are all the paintings ready then?"

Patrick's single nod was visible from her peripheral vision. "There's a lot of interest, and I'd bet this is the biggest show I've had since the gallery opened. It will be tough convincing him to do another."

"Why?" Almost done, three papers left.

"Because his muse is gone. He's barely talking about painting. In fact, he's more focused on his apartments than anything right now."

The paper was in her hand, and yet she'd heard an awful thing. "Murph, not painting? I can't imagine him not creating art."

"He's not really the same guy since you left. A lot of things have happened. Anyways," he held out his hand for the release, and she handed it over. "Not your problem. He's doing good, in my opinion. Just sucks if he gives up his talent, his dream."

"I'd agree."

"You should come to the show."

"He already showed me some of the paintings." In fact, thinking about them reminded her of her last night with him. So many horrible things happened in front of those beautiful canvases. "They were gorgeous."

"Did he show you the last one?"

"I don't think so. He was still working on it."

Patrick chuckled, folding the release and placing it

inside his coat pocket. "Then I really think you should come."

"Is there something I should know?" Dread filled her like there was some sort of inside joke she'd been left out of.

"He never told me you were real. He said he found a muse and the muse gave him the paintings. I believed you to be a figment of his imagination until the day you moved in. Then all the paintings made sense, but most of them missed some essence of you. These last ones have blown all the ruined ones out of the water."

She gasped. "You mean all the paintings..."

No, he'd been joking before. "I thought he meant the style."

"What?"

"He'd asked me when I saw the picture in the bedroom what I'd think about a show full of paintings like that. I thought he talked about the style of paintings he did. He was talking about a show with paintings of me."

How typical of her not to put things together. Damn, if she didn't feel odd with this revelation, too.

"Let me guess, you want the release back?"

She shook her head. "No, I don't. I want him to have his show, and the canvases he showed me are amazing. If all of them, or even half of them look like those, then I can see why he's getting attention. He's really good."

"Really? And you..."

"Took some courses in Art History." She didn't brag about that bit since she'd taken them in an attempt to garner affection from her mother, a futile effort.

"Huh, aren't you full of surprises. I won't stick around and take up any more of your time. The show starts at seven in the evening and runs until ten. A lot of my buyers like to go out before coming by. It's bad luck if they don't."

Patrick opened the door and stepped into the cold. "Hope to see you tomorrow.

Then he left, leaving her to think about Murph and his art. The man functioned fine without her, obviously. Sure, Patrick said he'd lost the will to paint. *Tell no lies. You left him without a muse.*

A guilt trip wouldn't work, and yet she wanted to ask him herself. Would he really let her stop him and his genius? She'd tell him off if that were the case. If they could survive without one another, then they could still do the things they were best at.

Then she realized that going to the show would be a temptation and the exact opposite of everything she'd promised herself. Things like, they needed to save themselves. They needed to own their problems, hold themselves responsible for fixing them. Patrick never mentioned if Murph had done that.

Risking everything to go back, even for the show, would serve no purpose except to destroy any hope she had.

Chapter Fourteen

Aggie tried not to think about the show. She really did. First, she scheduled a therapy session on Wednesday night. Then her therapist canceled, his wife was having a baby and checking into the hospital to be induced. So, dinner plans with a coworker, only the single mother's babysitter couldn't watch the baby because of the flu. The universe appeared to be working against her.

Then she decided to stay in and make Greek Moussaka like her father used to create for holiday meals. But she couldn't stop thinking about him…Murph. Maybe he didn't need to be perfect. He'd never be fixed. He loved her just the way she was, even committed to kissing her with puke breath. Seeing paintings didn't mean they needed to jump each other's bones. *Friends support friends.*

Before she could talk herself out of it, she put on her dark-red winter coat and headed out to the gallery. She hadn't bothered to get out of her work clothes or clean off her makeup, deep down knowing she wanted to go.

The show haunted her dreams as much as that last night with Murph now. She half expected him to be kneeling on the floor when she arrived, begging him not to take away his work.

Parking proved a pain, and she finally settled for a spot a few blocks away. The car beeped as she locked it and headed in the direction of the Blue Gallery. People milled out on the sidewalk, which she thought odd. Others were dropped off by cabs or friends who needed to park the car.

"Is there a line?" she asked a gentleman and his wife, judging by the way they clung to each other.

"No, head on in. It's a little hot in there because of all the people so we stepped out for some fresh air."

She opened the door, and the heat escaped, along with the scent of apples. Patrick had made sure the room smelled delicious. The first thing she saw was the painting from the bedroom, front and center. With the name of the exhibit as Murphy told her weeks ago, A Study in Emotion.

"Isn't it a marvelous exhibit?" an older lady to her left said to a companion as they walked by.

"Yes, I already purchased one of the paintings, but I may need another."

More comments like those swirled around her. The images of her and their creator were a success. A wild success, judging by the sold stickers positioned at each one as she started her circuit. She could tell the older paintings from the new ones. Each labeled with a different emotion underneath, but no matter the painting, she saw a different side of herself. Like snapshots in time as Murph visually provided images spanning years of her life. From the time they'd met, she'd inspired him to create.

It made her ache for the destroyed paintings.

"You came." Patrick came to a stop beside her. "What do you think?"

She glanced at him, all suited up in a pinstripe

ensemble with his black hair slicked back, the blond highlights were new. "About your hair or the show?"

"Funny, you make jokes." His smile disappeared. "The show, of course. My hair needs no validation."

"I love it. Where's the artist?"

"Of course, you'd ask me. He's mingling. Exactly where, I don't know since I've been dealing with purchase requests all evening. At this rate, we'll be sold out by nine. The good news is several patrons want to hire Murphy on commission."

"Really?" Commissions were a big deal, an important deal. After tonight, he'd no longer be a starving artist.

"There's the buzz floating to these ears. So, get your fill of these paintings tonight. Tomorrow, they won't be available." Patrick left her then, called over by someone else, no doubt to make another purchase. She continued moving slowly through the crowd, taking the time to look at each painting. Finally, she reached the ones Murph had shown her the night she called everything off.

Each picture brought a new tear to her eye, and she reached into her coat pocket for the tissue she'd placed there earlier. Dabbing at her eyes, she turned her head, and the final painting hung there large and imposing. She gasped, loud enough that several patrons looked at her. A couple of them did a double take, and she chose to ignore it.

This had been the painting he'd worked on in her bedroom. She was nearly naked then. He'd left the sheet covering her, everything white compared to her olive flesh. Her hair spread out on the bed in a chaotic fan pattern. The look on her face belied complete happiness with herself and her body, like she never experienced uncomfortable thoughts in her skin or found herself dissatisfied with her curves.

This photo showed a woman in love with herself as much as life. How he'd seen this part of her without her even knowing it existed boggled her mind. Even now, she wanted to reach out and touch the woman in the painting. To meet her.

"Excuse me, miss?"

Aggie turned to face the man tapping her on the shoulder. "My wife and I are in a debate over whether or not you're the model for the paintings. Would you care to help us settle the wager?"

She wiped at her eyes, a fresh set of tears replacing the previous ones. "I'm sorry. Give me just a minute."

"Not a problem at all. I'll admit, I'm more enamored by this last one than any of the others. It's so precious to capture the pure joy in existence, and exceedingly rare for an artist to do so."

Sniffling, she responded, "I agree. It's hard to capture for sure."

"One would almost say the artist would need to be in love and extremely close to the model to fully embrace the emotions he or she were trying to depict."

The words 'be in love' hit her hard. He hadn't been lying. No, this painting, if anything, confirmed his feelings and she'd tossed them aside.

"A very astute observation. You haven't seen or met the artist by chance?"

The older gentleman gave her a sad smile. "No, I'm afraid not."

Damn. And the crowd appeared to have gotten bigger. The possibility of finding him grew slim. "Do you know if anyone has bought this painting yet?"

"No, dear. This one has a special reserve price. Only the gallery owner knows what it is, and so far, no one has met it." He patted her on the shoulder. "You are the model, I presume?"

She nodded in agreement before wiping her cheeks and nose with the tissue. "Yes, and I have to find Mr. O'Shea, Murphy."

"If I see him I'll let him know you're looking for him."

"Thank you." She tucked the used tissue back into her pocket. Next time she saw Patrick she'd tell him he needed more wastebaskets.

"No, thank you. I won the wager, and now my wife won't get to choose our dining venue tonight." The older gentleman wandered off, and Aggie took a moment to try to look around the crowd. Her height gave her some advantages, and she could see over a good portion of the attendees. Then she caught sight of dirty blond hair, on a bearded face. *Hot Jesus*. He stood halfway across the room talking to Patrick.

The gallery owner pointed in her direction. Their eyes met, and she couldn't move. No, courage fled, and she stood torn between butterflies in her stomach and the sudden urge to seek help. Any help. This conversation...she'd have to apologize, maybe even beg. The one thing she'd have to do is tell him she loved him.

Thinking those words gave her an extreme case of anxiety. Patrick had said he'd been fine. What if he cured himself of whatever love-crazed emotions were driving their spark in the first place?

He started walking toward her, and all rational thought fled—no, all thoughts did. All she could do was drink in her fill of him. The facial hair was very becoming, but the circles under his eyes worried her. He'd dressed up for the event, wearing a three-piece suit and even combed his hair, which appeared to be growing out like crazy. Hell, his shoes were polished to shine.

She couldn't take this Murphy, not in all his finery and oozing sexual appeal. The glances of the women around him as he walked by confirmed her evaluation, Murph dressed in a suit equaled estrogen overload.

When he finally reached her, she held her hands out to him, and he clasped them with his own. The touch sent a tingle down her spine.

"Hi," the greeting came out whispered.

He leaned in, inches from her lips and whispered back, "Hello."

* * *

HE DIDN'T KNOW how to react, what to say or do. She'd come. Maintaining his distance, he kept one eye on her movements. She looked at the paintings, sipped water while staring at them, her eyes crinkling with her smile at some points. In another moment, she touched her cheek, the spread of a light blush rising on her pale flesh. He yearned to go to her, to ask her for her thoughts, impressions...anything.

For the last couple of weeks, he'd been in therapy, on the medication, which proved promising. So far, the side effects were minimal. He'd taken steps to save himself, to get better, but still didn't think he was in the best shape for Aggie.

When Patrick returned with the release, he'd peppered his friend with questions. She'd been in her relaxing clothes, sweats from her alma mater. Her hair had been up in a ponytail, and she'd been polite to him, asking how Murph was doing and if all the paintings were finished. Patrick volunteered information like his pledge to be done painting for a while, though his friend mentioned embellishing the story a bit. He didn't care, his thirst to simply hear anything about her overruled any other objections.

Patrick found him greeting another patron who offered congratulations and expressed interest in one of the paintings. He kept himself all smiles, humbled thanks, and then, his friend interrupted, begging forgiveness when he knew Patrick never gave a shit.

"She's here."

"I know," Murph replied. "I saw her come in, but figured I give her space. I'm not ready."

"I think she's had enough space since she saw Joy." His friend pointed in the direction of the final painting, his true masterpiece. The one Trix nearly destroyed. Thinking of the moment when she dove for the painting killed him. Then his eyes moved downward to Aggie. She looked at him head on.

"Go talk to her or I will. You're ready. You're taking steps." Patrick's words were coupled with a pat on the shoulder, most likely to instill courage, but the doubt and fear remained. There still existed a possibility she'd want nothing to do with him, maybe being on her own had changed her mind about her romantic feelings toward him. To talk to her would also mean, once again, revealing his feelings, though the paintings did that on their own.

"Fine, I will." He couldn't smile, not when his love stood across a room of people. She never broke eye contact with him, and he walked slowly, taking in every aspect of her visage. Her hair in some half updo, tendrils framing her face. A face red from crying, no visible tears, but something caused her pain. He only hoped his paintings were not a source, especially Joy.

Her red pantsuit and matching winter coat were a perfect contrast to her skin and hair. The light makeup, not super noticeable, but added just the right touch. If he held

Painting For Keeps

a sketch book or a canvas, he'd start working on a new painting now. He'd always want to paint her.

People parted as he passed, and he noticed the gathering audience, though he couldn't stop moving toward her even if someone told him it would be a horrible idea. He hated bringing attention to her, by now the resemblance to Aggie and his model for the portraits would have been recognized. No doubt they'd be swarmed. Then she held her hands out to him.

He clasped her cold palms within his warm ones.

Her whispered, "Hi," like a burst of sunshine against a winter chill.

"Hello," he whispered back.

For a moment they stood there, and he let people watch them. Let them ponder, wonder, and make inferences about Aggie. Then he finally couldn't stand the white noise around them. He wanted her to himself.

"Do you care if I get you out of here?"

"Where would we go?" she asked with a smile, making her eyes sparkle.

"Your car, Patrick's office, anywhere. There are things to be said." He had a dozen things to tell her. A month apart would do that to a man.

"I have things I need to tell you, too."

At that moment, he knew whatever direction they headed, a swirl of speculation would follow. Patrick believed drama made paintings sell, so he'd give them a whirlwind of it.

"Come with me." Without letting go of her hand, he moved them through the crowd and into his friend's office, which left nothing to the imagination since clear windows lined the office instead of walls. But the good news, a door with a lock existed and they got to be alone. He released her once they were inside, and when he turned, she stood halfway across the room. He secured the door and refused to pay any attention to the people outside. Instead, he faced Aggie and grinned, "I missed you."

She sniffled. "I missed you, too. Damn, I might cry again."

"Why?"

"Because you're gorgeous and everything...those paintings, you never showed me all of them. You never showed me the last one."

"After you reacted so horribly when I suggested paintings of you on display, I didn't know if you'd let me show it, since you're practically nude."

"Murphy, if you refused to display it, then it'd be a crime. And I would have never let you hide it from the world."

He froze, stunned by her response. "Really?"

"Yes, and all the other paintings capture exactly what you said they did. That's me looking at them objectively without identifying myself as the model."

They both laughed, and then they tried to talk at the same time.

"Murph—"

"Aggie—" He motioned to her. "You go first."

"I'm sorry. So sorry for our last night. I shouldn't have said the things I did. I should've been willing to give you another chance as we were. You never asked me to be perfect, but took me, loved me as I am. I don't want you to think I can't deal with your issues or accept them as a part of you. I love you, too."

He reached down and pinched the back of his wrist.

"What are you doing?"

"Making sure I'm not dreaming."

She smiled at him. "I promise, you're not. Every single

one of those paintings is selling out there, and Patrick mentioned people want you for a commission."

Nothing mattered beyond this moment. Aggie said she loved him. "I don't care."

"What? Don't be ridiculous—"

"Do you mean it?" He walked to her like a tiger on a hunt, corralling the prey.

"You'll need to be a little more specific than that."

"Do you love me?" He reached her and her chest heaved, breaths more like pants. She appeared as nervous and pent up as he.

"Of course, I meant it. Wouldn't say it if I didn't."

Goodbye to the last of his restraint, his resolve...all broken and shattered beyond recollection, so he kissed her. The roaring applause outside the office was too much to be ignored and they broke apart to bow to their audience.

"I can't believe our public display of affection was witnessed by everyone," she clung to him, not letting him go and he loved it.

"Well, Patrick told me if I wasn't going to actively try to sell my work, I should provide something to the show."

She let out a laugh.

Then he remembered. "Before anything else, because damn it, I want to kiss you again, I need to tell you, you're right. I can't keep up this behavior and rely on someone else to get me out of my upper and downer episodes. So, I signed up for therapy again. I'm on meds, which are working. I'm sticking to the diet and have come to realize that we have to be our own personal savior."

"What prompted this?" The glimmer of admiration in his eyes was worth every word of confession.

"Your words, and finally Trix. She had a total meltdown, nearly destroyed Joy and I almost let her. If it'd been any other painting—let's say getting Trix help meant I needed to get me help."

"Is she okay?"

"Nothing a short psychiatric stay won't fix, I hope. Seth is staying with me in the meantime. So, as long as you don't mind a little visitor, I've got an old bed I'm willing to throw out for a princess monstrosity." He hoped this wouldn't be a breaking point.

"I don't mind at all."

"So, what does this mean exactly?" Best to place the ball in her court, he wanted everything. Hell, if she needed it, he'd propose marriage and take her to the courthouse in the morning, but if anything, she'd want to move slowly.

"I'd say I'd like to come home in six months when this lease is up if you let me. Give us time to continue therapy, keep working on ourselves. In the meantime, how do you feel about being a soon-to-be-famous artist with a girlfriend?"

He pulled her against him again, kissing her lips with a soft, sweet touch. "I'd rather be the starving artist with the too-gorgeous-nutritionist-girlfriend."

"Looks like we'll both be getting what we want."

Epilogue

Six months later

Aggie walked into Cupid's Café, searching for Murphy among the booths and bean bags. Since they'd reconciled, the pair spent many an afternoon or evening at the place that provided them with a second chance. Between work, Murph's art commissions, and Seth coming into their lives, things were always busy.

"Welcome back, Ms. Kakos," said Angel, the café manager. This was the customary greeting he always offered her, along with an open hand.

Aggie shook his in response and tried to look around him to see if she could spot Murph, but the manager moved to block her path.

"I sense a little apprehension in you today. Is there anything we can help with? No one should feel uncomfortable in Cupid's Café."

The emotions he mentioned assembled in her body, a rioting, swirling mess of fear, doubt, and sense of déjà vu. She'd put herself out there like this before and gotten burned. Here she stood, willing to take the chance again. To continue what they'd started since her and Murph agreed to be together.

"It's just—"

"Say no more," Angel brought a finger to his lips. "But know that Mr. Heart and those of us at the café know all about taking chances and risks. We wouldn't set you up for failure."

She wanted to ask him how he had any clue about her thoughts, or the letter, but didn't get a chance because that's when she spotted her boyfriend.

"Aggie, over here!" He called out to her and waved from a booth on the far side of the windowed wall. If memory served, the same one they'd sat in eight months prior.

Angel stepped aside to let her pass and she headed for the one person who always looked at her as if she were the most gorgeous woman he'd ever seen.

"Hey, there, I was wondering what took you so long," Murph said as a he stood from his booth seat and motioned to her to climb in first.

"Sorry, the appointment took longer than expected."

"Well, your drink is still hot. I just got here." He pointed at the steaming cup of coffee.

The two gold hearts on the outside a reminder of what she intended to do next, after she took a sip of her beverage. The coffee went down smooth, warming her throat. "So, over the phone, you said you had good news."

"Yes, Trix signed all the papers and the judge has approved my petition. I'm officially Seth's guardian." The smile on his face made her want to smile as wide and big. The last few months had been a huge transition for the pair of them, but Seth was adapting well. Murphy had them both in therapy twice a week and Aggie had even joined them from time-to-time. Though Trix remained in a long-term mental care facility, he hoped one day she'd be able to be with Seth again.

"That's awesome news. Does he know yet?"

Murph shook his head. "Not yet. I planned to tell him this evening after his therapy session. I'm taking him out for a special dinner and hoped you could join us."

"I'd love to, but I've already got plans." She held strong, letting the words settle in. Normally, she'd never keep secrets, but this time she wanted to surprise him. Murph looked a little crestfallen, since they shared all the big days together. Birthdays, holidays, even Christmas and New Year's served as a big to-do. The merging of not just two, but three lives, and now it was time to take the last step. "I can't go to dinner because the movers are packing my stuff. I'm coming home."

"What? But you never submitted your thirty-day notice."

"I kind of forgot to mention that I did. You were busy getting ready for your show last week and finishing those commissions. Then I decided it would be easier to surprise you."

He leaned in and pressed a quick kiss to her lips. "It's the best surprise. Not only is Seth getting some stability, he's getting another person who will take care of him, too. You'll finally be where you're supposed to be."

"Where I want to be."

"Yes, now the only question is: when are you going to marry me?"

Aggie grinned. "We'll have to see, won't we?"

About the Author

Landra Graf consumes at least one book a day, and has always been a sucker for stories where true love conquers all. She believes in the power of the written word, and the joy such words can bring. In between spending time with her family and having book adventures, she writes romance with the goal of giving everyone, fictional or not, their own happily ever after.

Join Landra's Mailing List:
http://eepurl.com/bdKi9H

landragraf.com/

Note from the Publisher

Thank you for reading the Painting For Keeps. If you liked the stories, please leave a review. Reviews help the authors more than you know.

If you'd like to know more about After Glows, check out our website or email us at admin@AfterGlowsPublishing.com.

To stay current with upcoming titles, new releases, and other publishing news from After Glows subscribe to our **MAILING LIST**.

Also, join our Facebook Reader's Group to interact with our authors and other readers.

Thank you again for purchasing and reading Painting For Keeps.

Made in the USA
Lexington, KY
16 July 2017